I0642399

Callused Hands

Stanley Gazemba

First Edition: December 2013
Published by Nsemia Inc. Publishers (www.nsemia.com);
Oakville, Ontario, Canada

Edited By: Sheena Brennan
Cover Concept & Illustration: Stanley Gazemba
Cover Design: Danielle Pitt
Layout Design: Kemunto Matunda

Note for Librarians:
A cataloguing record for this book is available from
Library and Archives Canada.

ISBN: 978-1-926906-32-4

Acknowledgements

I started working on this story while employed as a casual hand at a cut-flower farm in Kiambu, Central Kenya. That farm very much resembled the one depicted in this story. The working conditions in this fictional story are the same as those I worked in: slave-like, brutal on the spine and lungs with meagre pay. The only way we could earn a better wage was by enlisting as night-guards on the farm in addition to day-long back-breaking labour.

It is not to say that being a night guard was any easier choice. When thieves came for the greenhouse lights and water pumps in the middle of the chilly wintry nights they usually chopped off heads of the guards they came across.

This story is dedicated to all the gallant lads of that place and time who braved it all, and still found it in their hearts to laugh off the misery in the village beer halls in the evening before retiring. It is dedicated to all the women who miscarried bended double in the greenhouse rows all day. I tried to tough it out, but in the end I wasn't tough enough to withstand the highland malaria.

You are all heroes for crunching on the giant wheel of progress without faltering, despite everything that is thrown at you.

Gazemba S. A.
Gikuni Village, 1993.

About the Author

Stanley Gazemba was born in Vihiga, Western Kenya in 1974. He is the author of *The Stone Hills of Maragoli* (winner of the 2003 Jomo Kenyatta Prize for Literature) that has been described by the *African Review* of Books as '...a book to watch in the century.' He is also the author of *Ghettoboy* (shortlisted for the Kwani? Manuscript Prize). He has also written several books for children and young adults.

Trained as a journalist, he has written for *Sunday Nation, Saturday Nation, The East African* and *The New York Times*. He is currently working as a regional editor with *Music in Africa*. His fiction has appeared in several anthologies. He lives in Nairobi.

Callused Hands is his first publication with **Nsemia Inc. Publishers**.

Chapter One

The chill of the evening bit the traveling man to the bone, causing his frostbitten fingers to turn white, curling like claws around the load slung over his shoulder. But even as the rawness of the mid-year winter assailed him through his thin clothing, he was more concerned about his wife Njambi, who was trudging wearily a step behind him, clutching the old greatcoat he had draped about her shoulders. In the stillness of the winding deserted country road hemmed in by towering wattle and gum trees he could hear her teeth chatter.

The fog hung around them thick and grey, driving against their naked faces in billowy clouds from the direction of Limuru yonder across the rolling ridge. It was hard to see anything twenty meters down the winding earth road, so they kept their ears open, walking along the side in case a vehicle came speeding out of the thick mist ahead.

"Yakobo, we should stop to rest," said his wife, leaning against a gum tree sapling. "I can't go any further."

He turned back and walked to where she was, lowering the old sack.

"How is it?" he asked fearfully, conscious of the rapidly falling dark. "Is the pain coming back?" He had hoped they would make it to the shopping center before dark, where they could find a place to spend the night before proceeding on their journey to Ngecha the following morning.

"It is all right," said the woman, smiling through

the pain etched in the deep lines on her brow. Her face was moist even in the evening cold. "I only need a little rest, that's all."

She looked unbelievably thin even through the patched wool greatcoat, the only fat thing about her the distended belly that strained against the coat buttons, causing her spine to curve inwards in the effort to support her advanced pregnancy.

"Here, you must take some tea," her husband said after he had settled her down on a sheaf of leaves. "It should keep you a little warmer." He rummaged in the old sack and took out a little flask that was encrusted with the grime of many years along the winding lines in the screw-on plastic base. He opened the flask with a little difficulty because he had screwed the top on tightly.

Pouring some of the black tea into a plastic cup, he raised it to her pale chapped lips.

She sipped slowly, the jutting veins in her neck bulging with every swallow, until the cup was emptied. He then poured some more and gave her the cup, which she cupped in both hands. As he screwed the top back on the flask, he shook it slightly to gauge how much of the tea remained. He craved for some himself, but he fought the urge.

They needed to use it well until they found somewhere warm to stop for the night.

As she rested against the trunk of the tree, he returned the flask to the sack and stood up to look around. He pulled up the collar of his faded wool coat, securing the huge wooden button on the collar. The coat bulged at the pockets with age and smelt of unwashed sheep as the mist settled on his shoulders.

He dipped his hands in the roomy pockets and studied the thick grey clouds, smelling the wet air. It

2

was only a matter of time before the icy drizzle started falling out of the gloomy sky. Such was the weather at this time of year the drizzle must escort the fog as they ganged up to keep the weak rays of the sun from reaching the land.

It would have been a lot easier with a roof over their heads, thought Yakobo as his mind wandered back to Gikuni, the little village where they had lived until that morning. Yes, it would have been better with a roof over their heads; even if they didn't have a glowing *jiko* to warm the tin-walled room or a meal to put in their bellies.

The events preceding their eviction from the one-roomed house were still vivid in his mind.

First he had lost his casual job at the flower farm where he had worked for three months. That had been frightening enough because by then Njambi had moved into his place, and the baby was due.

The landlord had accepted his explanation the first month as he struggled to put some food on the table doing odd jobs in the neighbourhood while he tried to get employment on another farm. In the second month, even the odd construction jobs in the neighbourhood became fewer and far between, and it grew increasingly difficult.

His patience running out, the landlord had turned up one day as they were away and put an additional padlock on their door. Yakobo had pleaded with the man, saying he had been promised to report to the farm the coming week. As days passed and the rent arrears piled up, the now unsmiling landlord sent two goons who ripped out the window, carrying it off.

Yakobo hung on, sneaking out at the crack of dawn and reappearing late at night. On the way back from his unsuccessful job hunt he would pass through the landlord's farm and help himself to a few cobs of green maize and some beans from the luxuriant garden, which he brought to his wife to cook. During the day he instructed her to keep away, and pass the time at her friend's vegetable stall at the shops.

Seeing as the tenacious tenant wasn't going to move out the goons returned with a crowbar and gouged out the door, ripping out one of the iron sheets at the spot on the roof above the spot where they spread the thin mattress on the floor.

"You don't want to break a leg for nothing, *Mzee*," they had warned tersely, brandishing the rusty crowbar in his face. "Please don't make us come back. Someone else is waiting to move in, and you are standing in the way. Go on, get out!"

They carted off their pickings into the night, the drizzle sliding off their long black coats.

It was the steeliness in their eyes that had convinced Yakobo they meant every word they said. He didn't plead with the landlord any more.

Lost in contemplation as he ambled down the deserted road looking for the nearest homestead, Yakobo heard the sharp scream. His heart leaping into his mouth he ran back to where he had left his wife.

Njambi was lying stretched out on the ground, her feet apart, legs jutting ramrod straight from underneath the old coat. Her moist face was contorted in pain, eyes squeezed shut, fists clenched around palm-fuls of grass and dirt she had gouged out of the earth.

"*Shhh... Shhh!* ... my love, I am here. It's okay. Be quiet, now...," he hushed, patting her frail shoulder. "Does it hurt now? Is it__."

The question died on Yakobo's lips when he saw the clear liquid on the ground between her feet. "*Ngai!*" he gasped, fear clawing at his heart.

4

He stood up and looked wildly about just as another painful spasm traveled up his wife's body, ending in another piercing scream that echoed through the trees.

Juma, the overseer at Chapa Kazi Farm, locked his leaning timber hut and stood outside, watching the farmhouse, which towered above the maize field.

The light in the TV room above the garage indicated the wealthy family was watching the evening news, seated around the blazing fire in the hearth. A little column of dark smoke wafted from the chimney, weaving languidly into the foggy evening air. There seemed no one else about.

He looked up at the gloomy sky, hanging thick with dark clouds, and wondered if the drizzle would hold until he got his loot to Ngecha. He was not worried about making his way back in the dark because at least he would have a few coins in the pocket. Also he would be fortified with a few tin-fuls of grain beer from the smoky shebeens of the township. And, who knew, maybe he would even have the company of one of the women to help him ward off the chill of the night.

With that reassurance, he buttoned his worn jacket up to the neck and blowing into his frozen hands, picked up the sack of tomatoes and onions and slung it on his shoulder.

He made his way cautiously through the maize field towards the trees, his breath trailing in condensed white puffs behind him. He hoped he would not run into one of the Maasai guards patrolling this *panya* route that the farmhands had created to avoid the main entrance. The guards would probably be huddled around their charcoal brazier at this hour, just like the farm owner JP. It was a rotten evening to be outdoors.

The drizzle started just after he got into the line of trees, pattering down in thin slanting droplets that felt like ice on exposed skin. As he approached the narrow passage cut through the rusty barbed wire strands that ringed that part of the farm he stopped, his ears cocked. He thought he heard a sound; a gasp like that someone in pain would make.

He listened keenly and heard it again, more clearly this time, coming from the thickets on the other side of the overgrown fence further up the road.

Puzzled, he set down his load and cautiously made his way through the bush, expecting a wounded man, probably robbed and left by the roadside. The country roads were becoming increasingly dangerous especially late in the evening, teeming with youths who couldn't find employment in Nairobi, and who had to earn a livelihood somehow.

The little head was covered with mucus, shiny and sleek. Through the film the few strands of hair plastered on the scalp were a rich dark colour. Yakobo crouched between his wife's spread legs and waited, his frostbitten hands cupped, praying that nothing would go wrong.

"Please try some more, Njambi," he urged, watching his wife's face, which was taut in concentration as she bit onto the saliva-wetted stick he had given her. "Try and push a little harder. It is almost out."

By then the confusion that had gripped him earlier on realizing he didn't know head or tail about childbirth had given way to a taut anxiety and a fright-filled sense of will. Somehow the delivery had to go well, regardless if he knew how or not. It just *had* to.

The only thing that rang through his mind was that he shouldn't *pull* the baby out; or if he had to, then he had to pull gently towards the mother's navel. He had seen animals aided that way.

It was as the blood-covered little bundle slid onto his shaking hands that he became aware of an added presence.

"There, there, *muthee*, I think you did it just fine," said the tall stranger, walking over to give a hand, a surprised smile slowly lifting the corners of his mouth. Just as the little fellow, on realizing he had exchanged the cozy warmth of the womb for a chilly noisy world shivered and opened his puckered little mouth, giving off a piercing cry of protest.

"He is a boy!" whispered Yakobo to the stranger, a boyish look lighting up his moist face. "*My* little boy!"

"Yes, brother. You are a lucky one too."

For a while they gazed at the noisy little thing, oblivious of the circumstances. It was plain that none of them knew exactly what had to be done next. That was before the stranger pointed out, "I think the lady there will need some cleaning, and the both of them will be cold too."

"You are right," said Yakobo, still talking in a whisper. "I wonder what comes next." He had fallen into an easy acquaintance with the stranger, as if they knew each other.

As for the other man, he was watching the dark little coil that trailed from the mother's birth opening to the baby, still giving it life. He was thinking of a cow he had once seen in similar circumstances, and how his father back in his village had handled it.

"Wait here a moment," he said, rising. "I think there is something we can do."

He disappeared into the trees the way he had come, and was gone for a while. Yakobo waited, a million thoughts coursing through his mind. In the

7

meantime he held the little thing tenderly, passing him carefully from one hand to the other, hushing him as softly as he could. He wondered why the little fellow could not be still.

The other man returned shortly with a 'blade' he had split off the skin of a broken maize stalk, together with two long grass blades.

With the grasses, they tied up the little umbilical cord in two places and prepared to slice it with the sharp maize-stalk splinter.

"You are sure about this, aren't you?" said Yakobo, warily.

For answer the other man grinned up at him, exposing a row of stained brown teeth. "Relax, my friend. It will be all right." Thereafter he got down to the little surgical operation, his strong farm-toughened hands shaking slightly.

"A little *jua-kali* it is, but that is how I remember my *Mzee* doing to the family calves," he said with a proud smile, passing the little package back to its father. "And they always grew into sturdy little studs too_ all of them!"

"Yes," said Yakobo, cradling the baby close to his chest, his hands still shaking with the anxiety that had gripped him. "And thanks you came along, *ndugu*. I really wouldn't know what to do exactly."

"Hey, you can call me Juma," said the other man, extending his hand for a firm handshake. "And as you congratulate yourself for a job well done, I think you should give thought to finding some clothing in which to wrap the little fellow. He will certainly freeze in this weather."

When the woman finally rose painfully to one elbow and opened her eyes, a weary smile spreading on her face, she found that they had already cleaned the baby as best they could with strips of clothing they tore off old shirts her husband had pulled out of the sack. Besides the pain and the hollow feeling in her belly, she reached for it and, with similarly trembling hands, brought it to her breast.

"*Ndonga*," she whispered weakly. "You want to kill me, you little thing!" Her face was stained with tears of joy.

"A nice-looking little fellow he is too," said the farm overseer, peering into the face of the crying little fellow. "I would be real proud of him myself, regardless of the surroundings he chose to make his entry into the world."

The woman smiled wearily up at the stranger, tears still streaming down her face.

They carried the baby through the by then darkened trees, pausing occasionally to allow the woman to catch up.

"I have some firewood in the house," said the farm overseer, leading the way. "We should be able to warm up the house for the night,".

The maize plants stood tall on either side of the winding path, their stalks green and supple with good health, broad leaves hanging with droplets of rainwater. Deep in the plantation the little hut of the farm overseer stood leaning at a solitary angle, walls covered with runnels of fine termite earth, shrouded in the fading light of dusk. A little courtyard surrounded the hut, overgrown with wet grass that encroached on the wooden walls. The man must live alone, thought Yakobo, cradling the now shivering tiny baby close to his chest.

Juma fished out a rusty key and fiddled with the rusty Diamond padlock, which gave at the third try.

He pushed the thin door inwards with a little creak of rusty hinges.

"*Karibu!*" he said.

They waited for him to find the lamp and strike a match to it. Then they sat down, the woman on a lone folding chair and Yakobo on an old oil drum that had been sliced in two and upturned to form a seat.

As Juma busied himself breaking twigs into the cold fireplace Yakobo handed the bundle to his wife and looked around. The single bed set against the wall was old, covered with a threadbare brown blanket. In the corner at the foot of the bed were stacked a few utensils atop a metal trunk with a warped top. Hanging on the wall beside the door was a smoke-stained framed black-and-white photo of the owner as a young man, standing proudly beside a pot of plastic flowers in the village photographer's studio. A thick kite's plume was stuck behind the picture, framed by two long porcupine quills like spears. They were tinged with black soot just like any other item hung on the walls. The black grainy soot hang from the tattered cobweb threads on the roof in thin long tendrils.

Selecting more wood from the bundle leaning against the wall, the host broke it on his knee and added it to the blazing fire, whistling in satisfaction.

"Thank God the fire lit easily. Sometimes the wood is wet and you have to coax it for a while, blowing inside until your eyes run," he said, rising off the hearthside stool and inviting the woman to move closer.

"Very rotten weather indeed," said Yakobo, drawing his drum closer to the fire to warm his hands.

"Ah, but it will be alright now that we have a fire going," said the other man, rubbing his hands together. "The little one should be able to keep warm throughout the night."

"I hope we don't finish your wood," said Yakobo, eyeing the little pile. "Dry wood should be quite precious at this time of year. I am sorry we budged in on you unannounced."

"Ah, don't you mind about that, my friend," said the other man with a broad smile. "There is lots of wood on this farm! I only need to go into the tool shed behind JP's house to replenish!"

"Thanks for taking us in for the night, all the same," said Yakobo. "My wife and I would hardly have made it to Ngecha, anyway."

"Ah, that's a little matter, my friend," said the host with a wave of the hand. "I'm sure you would have done the same if you were in my position. Now, I'll just fetch my load that I left outside, and then we'll make something to eat. I am sure you two must be hungry. It is quite a distance from the village. The lady will also want to clean u, no doubt." He fetched a huge old *sufuria* and placed it on the fire, balancing it on the three huge stones. He poured in some water from the jerrycan in the corner. "There is a bath shelter behind the house. You will find a bar of soap inside."

"You are most kind, my friend."

"Don't mention it, *bwana!* It is quite a while since I last had visitors, anyway. And guess what, you folks turn up with a bright little bundle too…it is a double blessing indeed!" his huge teeth flashed brightly in the orange glow of the fire. "Now, just you feel at home. I am afraid there are just the three of us in the midst of this huge maize plantation- rather a solitary life you will agree with me!" He extended a hand for a handshake. "Please feel welcome, my friends."

"I am Yakobo," said Yakobo in introduction. "My wife and I were on our way to Ngecha to seek out some relations to put us up for a while. You see I lost my former job, and now I have to search around."

"Is it?" said the host, his brow lined. *"Tch! Tch!* It is a bad thing, especially now with this little fellow to take care of."

"Yes, it is," said Yakobo, a little uncomfortably. "But then, what else does a man do but go out and look. I am confident I will find something in the course of the week. It is a good thing that you came along out there all the same."

Juma stood a while, gazing speculatively into the blazing fire, stubbly chin resting on a callused index finger that ended in a chipped encrusted nail. Then he tut-tutted like before and went out of the hut.

"He is a good man," Njambi spoke for the first time, cradling the baby by the fire, steam rising off the old wool greatcoat now that they were inside the warm hut. Outside the drizzle pattered on on the rusty tin roof, stopping for a while and starting again.

After Njambi was bathed and changed and the baby sponged clean, they sat around the fire eating the boiled green maize and beans Juma had made, washing it down with hot tea. "It is a pity it is all we have to welcome the little boy into the world," said Juma brightly. "We must see to it tomorrow that we slaughter a fowl and celebrate in the proper manner! The hot foul soup is really what the lady needs at this time anyway. It will help her get her strength back."

"Ah, we really do appreciate the meal, Juma," said Yakobo. "It is good enough, believe me."

"Ah! That is nonsense, *bwana!* This little *ndume* here deserves better!" said Juma, removing a fleck of corn that had wedged in his teeth. "And you know what? I've been thinking; maybe you aren't going to Ngecha after all. Yes, with the morrow, we'll have to see if we can get you something to do on the farm, Yakobo. I am sure JP will be willing to take you on to help with the work here. I'll talk to the man - he always has my ear."

"Juma."

His protestation was drowned in his host's laughter, which filled the little hut, adding to the warmth of the glowing fire.

After they had eaten, Juma further insisted on putting them to bed in his own bed across the room. "I will be fine down here on the floor, my friends," said the kind host. "I will be perfectly alright curled up by the fireplace. In any case that is where I used to sleep before I bought the bed!"

And as they sat a while later by the fire talking, the baby suckling softly underneath the thin blanket, cuddled next to its mother, Yakobo felt the warmth of human kindness wash over him as he gazed into the other man's clear eyes. Especially coming after what they had gone through in the village, and the cloud of uncertainty that had hung over him as they traveled on the deserted road.

Outside the drizzle pattered on the slanting iron roof, punctuating the ripening night with its droning music.

Chapter Two

The mist hung thick over Kampi Nyasi settlement. The first rays of the weak rising sun pierced the jagged strips of cloud that shredded the pale eastern sky as the faint ball prepared to peek over the line of ridges on the periphery.

The workers rose from the cluster of wooden shacks straddling the misty river and joined the throng on the cold path dissecting the village, headed for the creaky bridge that crossed the mud-coloured river, linking the village to the estate. The children scampered amidst the adults, shivering from the morning chill, stifling yawns in their palms, their sagging heavy sweaters wrapped tightly about them. The tins and other containers they used on the job swung from strings tied around their necks like burdensome appendages that must nevertheless not be left behind. One after the other they were swallowed into the coffee estate, which spread in a carpet of green up the hillside out of sight.

Yakobo poured a measure of the strong-smelling brown fungicide into the measuring cup and angled it against the morning light to check the level on the scale marked on the stained plastic. When he added it to the water in the old steel knapsack sprayer it turned a milky colour, spreading in languid tentacles towards the bottom of the drum. He added another measure and stirred with a stick until the water was an even milky colour. Then he rolled back the sleeves of his old sweater and the leggings of his trouser and lifted the heavy sprayer onto his back, swaying a little as he harnessed the nylon straps. He paused to still a bout of coughing that had been brought on by the effort, cupping his hand over his mouth.

Ka-chang! Ka-chang! Ka-chang! Ka-chang….!, went the familiar hand-pumping mechanism as he filled pressure into the tank, a task he remembered well from his work on young rose and carnation saplings on the flower farms. And with the building pressure in the tank the milky contents started trickling out from underneath the loosely fitting top, drenching the back of his worn sweater and spreading slowly at the base of his spine. Angling his cloth cap on his head, he picked up the nozzle handle and entered the first line, startling the gossamer-winged aphids hiding underneath the green leaves with a bust of the fine spray.

It was as he was coming back, working on the opposite side of the long line that he saw the beat-up jeep drive down the winding road that cut through the estate. It drove up to a stop beside where he had left his working equipment and a hefty man heaved himself out of the driver's side. Juma, who had been riding in the back, hoped down to the ground, waving at him to come over.

Yakobo unslung the nearly emptied tank from his back and ran, hastily brushing his white chill-bitten palms on his pants.

J. P. King'ong'o took a few gouty steps around the front of the truck and stopped, leaning against the rusty bulbar. Taking off the fine leather Stetson, he swiped at the moisture on the band with a forefinger, and then he wiped his forehead with the pink meaty palm and replaced it. He was a stout middle-aged man, not very tall, and whose well-fed paunch hang low, putting strain on the thin leather belt that struggled to hold his pants above his rotund hips. He looked every inch a man who had either made or inherited his wealth early in life, and who enjoyed every penny of it with every passing day. But his shifty little eyes, as he got closer, also gave the impression he was equally determined to hold on to it.

"*Jambo!*" he said in the thin wheezy voice of a seasoned haggler at the local cattle market.

"*Jambo, Mzee,*" said Yakobo, conscious of the scrutinizing gaze sweeping slowly over him as he drew closer.

"You handle the sprayer rather well. Have you done this job before?" he said, scratching the base of his belly.

"Yes, *Mzee*. I know it well enough," said Yakobo, hoping his nervousness wasn't showing.

"You know how to mix the chemicals?"

"*Kabisa!*"

"Juma will show you how we do it here, all the same. I will be watching your work all the time. But just to warn you," he said, removing the hat and twirling it thoughtfully in his hand, "I don't tolerate lazy people on this farm. If I detect any sloppiness in your work I will throw you out, *umesikia*?"

"Yes, *Mzee*."

The farm-owner gazed into the distance a while, his squinted little eyes scouring the rolling expanse of the coffee crop. "What about mama? What does she do?" he said suddenly.

17

"Er... she can do practically everything, *Mzee*... she can pick coffee, weed the lines, and any other work you may have, *Mzee*."

"That's good. I understand she cannot work at the moment, eh? You are a proud father now, is it?" There was a look of slight mockery in his eyes. "All the same I expect her to be working in two months' time. I have a shortage of staff at the cherry factory, and seeing as picking will be heavy in a few weeks time, I expect her to help. I won't have her staying on the farm doing nothing, understand?"

"Yes, *Mzee*," nodded Yakobo eagerly.

"Alright, go back to your work. We'll talk about your wage at the end of the week."

"*Asante, Mzee*."

A wave of relief swept over Yakobo as he lifted the sprayer onto his back and adjusted the straps.

JP stood a while by the roadside, inspecting the crop. And then he turned and lumbered back to the jeep, heaving himself behind the wheel. Juma jumped into the back and they drove off in the direction of the river, where the mist was slowly lifting above the spread of workers foraging inside the coffee bushes.

***

The chilly weather lasted the better part of the month. The sun showed only occasionally, a dull glow that peeked through a slight part in the endless grey vault, and which would bring momentary reprieve to the dripping country underneath before it was swallowed back into the folds of the thick blanket. Towards the end of the month however the drizzly rains stopped and the mist grew less thick in the

18

morning. And then one morning the sky was clear and the warming rays of the sun pierced again from the distant ridges, strong and supple.

Further down in the valley along the mud-coloured river the *sukuma-wiki* and spinach patches, which had grown luxuriant in the endless drizzles, formed a knit patch of green. The paths cutting between them were straight and geometrical, a rich red in colour, like the soil of that part of the country was.

The old women who tended to them bent low over the luxuriant patches, filling their huge *ciondo* baskets, which they then lugged onto their stiff backs, passing the wide band stretched over their foreheads. They trudged all the way to Kampi Nyasi where they hawked them from door to door.

This was the flip side of the dour weather. Now the *sukuma-wiki* was in plenty, and the milk vendors had to literally beg the villagers to buy.

In the light of the dying day Yakobo and Juma were busy at work, nailing planks onto the wooden structure they had put up at the spot where JP had shown them, deep in the maize field about fifty yards from Juma's house. The planks were thick with moisture, almost going to rot.

Seeing as he had no use for them, JP had allowed them to select what they needed from the rotting pile in the yard behind his house.

And, somehow, they had juggled the odd pieces of off-cut timber until the house was complete. It remained only for roofing.

This was going to be a little tricky though, given the scraps of old iron sheet they had gathered from the scrap in the yard came in all shapes and sizes, and they were going to call for a lot of inventive posturing in order for the roof to be complete.

"Ai!" said Yakobo, stepping back to stretch his sore back. "Shall we really manage with these pieces of scrap?"

"I say, we shall do it," said Juma encouragingly, watching his friend as he too stepped back to assess their progress. "Don't you start imagining it is an impossible task, my friend."

"Tch! Tch! It is going to be real tricky with these scraps we have for material," said Yakobo, looking at the rusty pile.

"I tell you, just wait you'll see. How, anyway, do you think I managed to roof mine? Eh? It was from these same scrap metals! And there it is, still standing two years after!"

Yakobo looked across the maize field at his friend's house, leaning at an angle, roofed with flattened out pieces of rusty tin cans that were nailed such that they overlapped one another like earthen tiles. "It must have taken you a long while to finish the roof."

"That it would. Fortunately it was in the drier months, and I had some young men from Kampi Nyasi come to give a hand. But still we had to cut and flatten out the tins one after the other, not to mention do all the nailing using rocks. You see I had no tools then," said Juma, laughing at the memory.

"It must have been tough work, tut, tut...," said Yakobo, scratching an itchy spot on his arm where a rusty tin end had caught him. "Anyway, let's see what we can do tomorrow then." He started gathering the tools and twisted nails scattered all over, putting them in an old oilcan. "As for now, I guess a bath is in order.

And then we'll visit Mama Pima down at Kampi Nyasi. The drinks are going to be on me today."

"You really have taken a liking to the place, haven't you?" said Juma with a grin. "That old mama sure makes really strong stuff."

"I guess it must be the ingredients that go into making the liquor that count. Someone once told me they add a field mouse- the tiny *mbeva* type that have black stripes on their fur- into the drum at the fermenting stage to make the drink *kali.*"

"Oh, no, my friend, you heard wrong," said Yakobo, tears glistening in his eyes with laughter. "I know of an old hag who would wring the barley waste inside a soiled piece of her underwear; and this was done when her new moon was standing overhead in the sky."

"Hey, hey, the woman will overhear you," cautioned Yakobo as they approached the house.

Njambi was sitting outside on a folding chair nursing the baby. When she saw them approach through the maize field she rose and went to get their bath water ready.

She had grown a lot healthier since they had arrived at the farm, her face bright with a new sheen; bust straining with fat and milk. It was hard to compare her to the wasted woman who had been overcome in the wattle trees by the roadside on that drizzly evening many days gone by.

It was getting fairly dark when the two friends, washed and changed, set off through the maize field in the direction of the river. It was a crisp evening, the cool breeze blowing from the tall gum trees at the edge of the field ruffling the luxuriant maize plants.

"There is going to be a good harvest from this field this season," said Yakobo, burying his hands in the roomy pockets of his coat.

"Indeed," said Juma, pausing in his off-key whistling. "JP is going to be a happy man. The seasons, it seems, were just right for the maize crop. You notice the rains stopped just as they were showing their crowns."

Yakobo gazed out at the vast expanse of luxuriant green straddling the hillside, and which was darkening as dusk settled. "You know, Juma, I find myself envying the man sometimes."

"Why so?" said Juma, yet again interrupting his whistling.

"I mean, all this land under maize, cabbage, thousands of hectares under coffee …and yet there's still lots more lying fallow! And yet look at us, we are virtually squatters, you and I, living at the man's mercy, making the land produce for him season in season out- I mean, it is unfair!"

"Yeah, you are right," said Juma, scratching at a corny growth on his nose. "You know, I've never quite thought of it in that way."

"It is quite unfair," said Yakobo, shaking his head sorrowfully. "Thousands of hectares for one man, and yet I don't even own half an acre myself!"

"It bothers you, doesn't it?" said Juma, not sure what had spurred the thought in his friend. "You know, personally, I try not to think too hard about things that are beyond my reach. I prefer to let things fall in place one by one; when the time is right."

Yakobo made an angry clicking sound and spat

on the ground, brushing a bent maize plant out of the way.

"You don't have a piece of land for yourself back home in Western?" said Juma, curious. "I thought every male was entitled to a slice of the family land. Me I have my portion waiting in Kaloleni, only I guess by now it must be overgrown with bush. My brother is putting it to use in my absence tapping the few palm trees on it for *mnazi* wine, which he sells to villagers. I guess one of these days I'll save up enough money and go back to develop it." There was a doubtful look on his face even as he said this.

"I have a piece of land myself too," said Yakobo. "A rocky strip that barely grows any maize. And indeed I put up a reed-thatched hut on it too. I guess by now the thatch must have rotted, same to the poles- that is if the hut is still standing at all! I had to come out here to seek employment because there was just no way I could sustain myself on the stony land."

"Better for you, my friend. Me I hardly have a *makuti banda* on my own- I am virtually homeless!" said Juma with a carefree laugh. "And so, you see we are all in the same boat here!"

"It is strange all the same, leaving your parcel of land to come and live as a labourer on another man's, to be kicked and insulted, and paid a pittance for your troubles."

"Look, Yakobo, I think you will only get your head all wound up thinking about these things," said Juma at length, wiping his watery eyes. "Let's go to Mama Pima's and enjoy our tipple for the day and come back to sleep. Tomorrow's matters we will worry about when the time comes, I say."

"You really have taught yourself to leave on the cheap," said Yakobo with a chuckle. "Just like all seasoned drunks."

"Heh-heh! My friend, you can't take on the world with your mere hands and hope to win! If you have no wealth then it is only advisable that you lie low and take what comes your way- trust me!"

Yakobo shrugged resignedly and followed his laughing friend down the path towards the river.

***

Back at the house, after the two friends had departed, Njambi sat rocking the child gently in her lap by the fire, cooing a lullaby her own mother had sang to her as a child. It was as she reached to brush an ashy speck that had landed on the child's cheek that she heard approaching footsteps outside. Shortly there came a knock at the door.

Thinking it was her husband who had forgotten something she laid the baby on their bed to one side of the hut, which was newly fashioned out of old timber and twigs, and went to open the door.

"Ah, *habari*, Mama!" JP looked radiant in a cream suit and an open viscose shirt, leaning against an ebony cane that had an image of a bull elephant carved into the handle. "Where is *Mzee*?"

"They left just now. I think they went down that way towards the river, said Njambi, gesturing with a finger. She was a little nervous all of a sudden, not sure if to welcome the farm owner into the hut. He was clearly the last person she had expected to come calling at the hour.

So far in their stay on the farm she had only seen him from a distance, either talking to Juma, or her husband about the work.

"I see! So they went off to have a drink of *chang'aa* in the village as usual, is it?" said the wealthy farm owner, a bright smile playing on his moist face. "Or is it they think I don't know? Ha-ha-haaa..." he broke off into reeling laughter, at the end of which he had to remove a pressed white handkerchief from his pocket and carefully dab at his watery eyes. "You see, I know about everything that goes on on this farm. My ears are long indeed! And that woman running the business thinks I don't...Ha, ha!" There was a callous ring to his laughter; as if he was inviting her to be privy to just one of the many secrets he kept in his head. "Well, let them amuse themselves. It is their money, after all!"

At a loss for what to say to the farm owner, Njambi smiled nervously and said, "*Karibu, Mzee.* We just had our evening tea. But I'll make you a cup, if you are not in a hurry."

"Ah, I'd love *that* at this hour, woman!"

JP lingered a while at the door, looking at the termite-infested walls. Then he tipped his hat and stooped underneath the eave, stepping into the smoky room. He stood a while in the center of the room as Njambi hurried to find a cloth to dust the folding chair.

In the fireplace the few logs in the hearth crackled softly as the breeze from the open door passed over them, fanning up a few tongues of orange flame that rent the darkened room in their fiery glow. Propped up on one of the cooking stones the little tin lamp struggled to hold onto its dying flame, which danced left and right to the sweep of the breeze. The cloth wick was running dry of kerosene. She would need to ask Yakobo for some money the following day to buy some down at the village.

"*Karibu!*" said Njambi again, presenting the now dusted chair. But JP stood still, leaning on his cane, examining the room.

"Seems like you have done quite a job beautifying this place, woman," he said at length, his eyes sweeping over the newly pasted old newspapers lining the walls. "It was in a rather messy state before. But now it resembles a home!"

"Thank you, *Mzee*," said Njambi shyly.

"Indeed it is orderly now. It is true what they say about the touch of a woman after all. Maybe Juma should learn from this and get a woman of his own to take care of the place now that you two are building yours." he said with a satisfied nod. "He should stop chasing after those old mamas in Kampi Nyasi who are no good for anyone!"

He ended with a bellowing laugh that rang in the confines of the little wooden house.

Across on the bed the baby stirred from sleep and gave a cry.

"Oh, ...Oh, sorry I woke the little one," said JP, looking towards the bed. "*Habari Toto*?" he called in the manner of a child.

"It is alright," said Njambi, going to fetch it. "It was his feeding time anyway."

"What do you call him?" he said, moving closer to peer into the baby's face. "Such a beautiful child he is too."

"Ndonga is his name," said Njambi proudly, raising the baby to her breast, rocking it gently in her arms. She sat down on the bed and shushed it, whispering at it to be quiet.

The wealthy man stood by, watching them, his cane planted on the floor between his feet. Seeing that the baby would not be quiet, she was forced to unbutton her dress and suckle it. A wave of embarrassment passed over her as she pushed the dark nipple into the noisy baby's mouth, conscious of the wealthy man's gaze fixed on her.

JP stood gazing a while, watching the silky brown of her full breast as the child suckled. Then he turned and prepared to leave. "I guess I should leave you now to suckle the baby, Mama Ndonga. He seems rather hungry...And my presence is obviously not needed. *Tukuonana rosho!*"

A strange feeling settled over the woman as she watched the wealthy farm-owner walk off into the maize field, shifting his enormous mass with effort on his sandaled feet. Then she got up and drew the door shut, before going back to sit by the fire.

Chapter Three

The general elections of that year found the coffee trees in flower, a sweet smell filling the air around the vast estate as the insects flitted busily from one bush to the other.

Most of the casual hands had been laid off by this time of year, awaiting the coming picking season when Kampi Nyasi would be bustling with life again. Only a skeleton staff remained to process and package the harvested produce.

Yakobo was working in the store, an old brick building with huge iron sliding doors and a rusty high corrugated iron roof built with a ventilation allowance at the apex, and which stood next to the cherry factory. His job was to unload the cherry from the pallet truck as it arrived from the drying yard and stack them in columns along the brick walls of the store.

Outside his wife worked with two other women, carrying the freshly hulled beans out to the field where they spread them on the long sieves built along the terraces on the slope all the way to the river. A hunchbacked old man carrying a white cane spread them out in the sun to dry, leaning across the terraces so he could push them to the far end. He moved along the drying racks with the familiarity of someone who had been working long at the place.

Njambi had widened considerably at the waist with the second pregnancy. Maybe it was due to the fairly good food they now enjoyed at the farm. Her cheeks were rounder and her eyes brighter too, quite unlike what she had looked like when she had carried Ndonga.

As for the boy, he sat perched on the wall enclosing the trough filled with murky brown water underneath the long metal spout issuing from the belly of the machine. He was watching one of the workers servicing the dormant machinery.

Often his mother had warned him to keep away from the machinery, but he paid no heed. He liked to come here especially when the harvest season came round and the machine was turned on. He was fascinated by the huge wheels and gears turning in the belly of the machine and the maze-work of bands and rods that connected them, all going with an oiled smoothness; and the belly-filling cling-clang that emanated from therein. It was amazing how this machine sucked up the river through the long steel pipes and belched it out down the other end into the oil-slaked channel that ran down slope. And yet it wouldn't have enough, for the clanging machinery still demanded more, gurgling noisily and ejecting it.

It must be a very greedy machine, thought Ndonga.

And yet its allure was such that every afternoon after he had had his lunch he would sneak behind the house and into the maize field, and then, before his mother knew it, he would be racing across the field and down towards the river to see it.

"Pass me that broom over there, *kijana*, will you?" said the service man, indicating the oily broom perched on the wall next to the spout. "Careful there you don't loose your footing and fall into the pit, or you will have no teeth left in your mouth to speak of," he cautioned as the boy rose.

Ndonga balanced on the rim of the pit and started edging towards the broom, his arms held out, the paper plane he had been holding gripped tightly between his clenched teeth. He took hold of the oil-slicked broom handle and started back, quite unafraid of losing his balance because the cement verge on which he stood was coarse. In any case he had often played up here with his friends.

"*Ehe*? And where will my teeth go to if I fall?" said Ndonga after he had handed over the broom, perching on the sharply angled edge.

"You really want to know?" said the service man, pausing to roll back the sleeves of his oil-stained overalls. "I suppose they will be knocked back down into your throat."

"Ha-ha-ha...! Now, *that*'s a lie," said Ndonga. "I am not a little boy to fall off such a wall that easily. In any case I would jump onto that pipe over there very fast like a monkey, if by any chance I were to lose my step."

"Very smart, eh?" said the serviceman, pointing a cautioning greasy finger at the boy. "I suppose you wouldn't be saying the same lying on your back on the white sheets in the hospital in Kikuyu listening to the skinny white sisters stitch up your scalp."

"*Woooi*! And just what would have happened to my scalp?" There was a look of mock horror on the boy's face.

"You don't know?" said the service man, crouching underneath the painted manifold so he could scrub the greasy deposit underneath the coiled pipes. "Of course you *wouldn't* anyway. Because that little skull that is hard of hearing would be cracked right open."

"*Woooi*!" cried the boy again, horrified. "You lie!"

"Is it? Do you know what the sisters put inside the skull of a little boy who has lost his brains?" persisted the man, laughing. "A sheep's brain, that's what.

Now, you don't want to start walking around going *baaa! Baaa!* Like a sheep, do you?"

And as the serviceman busied himself underneath the giant engine Ndonga stretched out on his belly on the top of the wall and watched.

Back in the brick building Yakobo had removed his shirt as the heat of the day built, and now he had folded it and spread it across his shoulders, on which he received the bulging sacks from the man perched on the pallet. Little step by step he climbed up the hill of sacks, taking it up to the top column at the far back.

"Perhaps you will want to finish your work a little earlier today, Yakobo," said his mate lounging on the pallet truck.

"Why?" said Yakobo shaking beads of sweat off his brow.

"I hear the *kijiji* is lively today. I heard there was someone dishing out money at Kampi Nyasi yesterday," shouted the other man from atop the pallet.

"Is it?" said Yakobo, lowering the sack with a practiced heave of the shoulder onto the others at the top, and bringing up his hand to swipe at his sweaty brow.

"A band of young men were spotted outside Mama Pima's house late in the day. It is said they called out Mama Pima and asked her how much of the liquor was remaining. They then settled for the price and asked that it be given free to everyone who was inside."

"I wish the free drink had found me there. Still it is hardly surprising, seeing as the election campaigns are gaining steam. I suppose a lot of money will be flying around." Juma settled on the sacks to regain his breath, fanning himself with a piece of cardboard.

"Those who are in the know say it is the time when

one should always be abroad and about, especially evenings. It is the season for men to desert their households and pitch tent at market places."

"I wonder who will be handling JP's matters this time around," said the other man, dragging on a stub of cigarette that didn't have a filter at the mouth end. "I heard he is going to run for a parliamentary seat."

"Well, no doubt he is going to recruit agents from amongst us."

"There is little doubt about that. We are his people."

"I don't suppose there will be much work on the farm starting next week. The picking is almost over now."

"I only hope the man opens up his fist a little wider this time. Last time he was full of empty promises. He even distributed iron sheets, food and *lessos* all over, trying to woo the voters in all the surrounding ridges. Do you know what happened after he failed to make it?"

"You tell me."

"Everyone was too busy in the drinking dens celebrating they hardly knew what was going on. The man went around with an old lorry, stopping at every household. He had the agents go in and recover all the free goods, which they lumped into the back of the truck. Even those who had already nailed them on their roofs were not spared, the sheets were forcibly removed and taken away, the owner lumped with abuse for having ruined *mheshimiwa's* property. The truck took them back to his hardware store in Kiambu, as for the ruined they went to do construction work on the farm."

"What a mean thing to do!" said Yakobo, appalled.

"I can say it with certainty because I was part of

the gang. It is true. You see, when you deal with JP, it's either he gets what he wants from you in return, or you don't get nothing at all. He must always win! You don't know the man, I tell you!"

It was as they were talking that a column of dust was sited down the winding road in the direction of the bridge.

"Well, seems like we spoke too soon," said Yakobo, cupping his hand over his brow. "Quick! Slide down that sack! You don't want the man catching us idling now, do you?"

JP's jeep drove fast up the road and drew to a stop outside the store. Juma jumped out and ran into the store. He was dressed in a new cap that was branded with the logo of the Axe Party, and his moist face was moist with excitement.

"You two will have to stop what you are doing. *Mzee* needs you to accompany him to an assignment in Ngecha," said Juma, wiping sweat from his brow.

"Hey, we were just talking about this!" said the other man, climbing down from the cart excitedly.

"The campaigns, is it?" said Yakobo, pulling on his shirt. "Any idea what's in store for us?"

"Oh, you will be well taken care of," said Juma with a grin. "*Mzee* is in a good mood today. Now, come on you two. We don't want to keep the *Mdosi* waiting, do we?"

They filed outside and climbed into the back of the jeep.

There were three other young men seated there in the back. They looked rather scruffy; their eyes reddened with what could only be an early drink.

This was soon evident as one of them pulled a jerry can from underneath the bench and opened it, shaking it against the light to gauge what was left inside. Raising it to his lips he took a long swig of the strong-smelling liquor, grimacing as the fire spread at the pit of his stomach.

Baring his brown-stained teeth in a hideous grin, he passed the jerrican around. "Come on, *wasee*, have a sip. It is for free!"

"Here, Maish! Pass over that *burungu*, man," said one of the lads, extending a ham fist that was adorned with a metal-studded leather wristband and a multi-coloured Maasai beaded finger ring.

A little bundle wrapped up in old sacking was resting at his feet and Yakobo couldn't help wondering what was inside. A chilly sensation stirred the pit of his stomach on realizing it concealed some crude weaponry.

Sitting upfront in the cab beside JP was a beefy man wearing a cloth cap, and whose round face was dark as coal, squinted eyes buried inside folds of flesh. He was smoking a well-polished wooden pipe.

As soon as they were all boarded JP engaged gear and they sped off with a shower of gravel, banging down the rutted road towards the bridge.

And as Joshua accepted the jerrycan from the youth called Maish and raised it to his lips, it dawned on him that they were onto a dangerous mission. Well, one might just as well fortify themselves a little. Especially seeing as the booze was in plenty, and for free.

They linked up with a band of other youth who were packed in the back of one of the old farm trucks parked beside the road that led to Gikuni. A young man climbed down from the truck and raced to the jeep carrying a little bundle, which he tossed in the back. They wore more of the red branded t-shirts and caps, which were quickly distributed around. The young man went round to the cab to talk to JP. Stuffing a fat brown parcel JP had given him inside his jacket, the youth ran back to the idling truck and climbed into the cab. The truck led the way, going in the direction of Gachie, the jeep following close behind.

They turned off the road just outside the shopping centre and drove into a bushy compound through the open rotting wooden gate. The vehicles drew to a stop in front of the old iron-roofed house and the youths leapt out.

An old man who had been lolling in a broken rattan chair on the verandah stirred and watched them through watery grey eyes. His skinny dog was not so bold in front of that rough-looking ensemble. Shooting them a diabolic stare, it rose and scampered away into the weedy flowerbed, tail tucked between wasted hind legs.

JP's passenger stepped out of the jeep and spoke to a scrawny beady-eyed youth dressed in a worn leather waistcoat and faded ski hat, who appeared to be the leader of the lot. From the nearby shops the murmuring of a noisy gathering could be heard, the piercing whine of the PA system jarring the stillness of the laid-back town as the organizers of the event set up the equipment at the dais.

The fat dark man was giving instructions on how he operation was to progress, but Yakobo was hardly listening. He was already feeling tipsy from the liquor. As the reality of what they were engaged in dawned back in the jeep, he had taken generously of the drink in the hope that it would embolden him more. The youth with the brown-stained teeth had said there was good money in it at the end of the exercise. That it was really going to be a piece of cake disrupting the campaign rally, knowing the weak security detail of the Dove Party candidate as he did. It was the ease with which the youth spoke that frightened Joshua, add to that hideous grin. All of a sudden he regretted having accepted to get into the jeep in the first place.

"*Wacha kuingiza baridi, mbuyu. Hii* job *ni* simple," the lad called Maish had quipped encouragingly, drawing from a spit-wetted strong-smelling roach.

"I say, this is a piece of cake!" encouraged Juma, grinning. "We have done this before, *bwana!*"

But still Yakobo was ill at ease.

The Dove Party had set up the dais in front of the pub, green banners draping the wooden dais emblazoned with the white emblem of a dove with an olive branch in its beak. Green was the dominant colour in the modest crowd that had gathered, the politician's youths strutting around in the new t-shirts and caps, waving tiny flags and working up the crowd in anticipation of their man.

The technician finished setting up the PA system and a troupe of *mwomboko* dancers who had been keeping the crowd entertained with their ancient step dance left the stage. The politician stepped out of the Land Cruiser parked close by and waved at the elated crowd, hoping up the creaky stairway onto the stage.

"Greetings the people of Gachie!" he thundered in his commanding bass, waving his white flywhisk, smoothing the designer silk suit over his protuberant belly. "I greet you in the fashion of the Dove Party!" He clasped both hands and raised them above the set of microphones, to which the crowd responded with a similar gesture, ululation s renting the air from the strings of rehearsed hecklers lined up at the front.

"Thank you! Thank you! *Asanteni Sana!*"

Flashbulbs popped all over as the few paparazzi journalists covering the event tried to get the best shots to take away.

"You know why we are gathered here today, don't you?" A choreographed roar greeted his words. "Well, for those who don't, I will tell you. We are here to break the haft of the axe!" a thunderous roar from the strategically placed hecklers greeted the pronouncement. "We are here to break the haft of the axe indeed! We are here to break the axe that has had a stranglehold on you people all these years. We are here to show a repeat of what we did last time. We are here to trample on years of abuse and poverty and usher in an era of prosperity by the dove! We are here to bring change to the lives of the people of Gachie!"

A roar of applause interrupted the speaker yet again, drowning out his voice even on the powerful PA system.

All of a sudden a band of red shirts spilled out of the alleys issuing all around the market square and surrounded the mob, slashing the air with their rubber *nyaunyo* whips, which curled above the crowd like black snakes before descending with a snap. In no time everyone was running in a panic, some screaming, others crouching on the ground, their arms clasped over their heads to ward off blows and stumbling feet.

…Twap! Twap!, rang the *nyaunyo* whips, scattering the startled crowd.

A red shirt raced towards the generator and snapped at the black power cord snaking from the noisy machine with rubber-reinforced pliers, cutting off the power. He attempted to cart off the generator, but finding it too heavy, vented his anger on the tinted windshield of the expensive Land-cruiser parked close by, shattering the glass with a vicious strike of the thick pliers head. Yet another red shirt ran around the car, smashing lights and mirrors with a rock.

In the centre of the stampede a fist-to-fist engagement had ensued between a band of greenshirts who had hurriedly ringed around the dais and the invading red shirts. Balled fists and kicks were flying helter-skelter, yells of pain punctuating the confusion as someone fell and scrambled out of the melee to escape stamping boots.

A red shirt streaked across the dais and snatched the cordless microphones from their stands. Another clambered up the nearby tree and ripped a loudhailer off the supporting nail, carrying it off into the alley behind the pub.

A group of green shirts gave chase, but they were repulsed by a fierce band of red shirts that had been crouching in the alley, guarding the loot.

Yakobo broke from the screaming crowd and made his way towards the alley where he had seen the youth with the loudhailer disappear. His earlier resolve had deserted him at the sudden eruption of violence. He could hardly locate Juma in the confusion. All he wanted was to get away back to the bushy compound where they had left the trucks. Rocks and other missiles were flying about, and it was dangerous standing still.

It was as he was nearing the narrow entrance that a foot stuck out in his way, tripping him. As he fell face-first with a grunt he had the presence of mind to roll over onto his back, feet raised in the air ready to kick at his adversary. A band of greenshirts, their eyes red-rimmed, loomed above him, their snarling lips bared for his blood. One of them was raising a broken wooden plank, ready to smash it on his head.

Yakobo gave a horrified scream, kicking helplessly about as visions of what they were about to turn his body into with their clubs filled his mind. But the next minute some of the red shirts who had heard his scream were pouring out of the alley, raining *nyaunyos* at his attackers.

Pushing between two of the lads, he passed into the dark alley and ran, ducking, but not quite avoiding the peppery lick of a curling whip on his back. He tore into the maize and bean fields behind the shop, intent on getting as far away from the chaos as possible.

He stopped at a trimmed kei-apple hedge to regain his breath and looked around, trying to regain his bearings. He was in the midst of maize and vegetable fields, hemmed in by trimmed hedges, in the midst of which stood the tiny wooden and *mabati* houses of the peasants. The maze work of tracks cutting through the village were narrow, just enough to accommodate a donkey-cart. He was also conscious of his branded red shirt and the danger it paused. In his naivety, he had left the shirt he had been wearing in the truck, not having the foresight to wear it underneath the red shirt just incase there arose the need to conceal his identity. He was not sure if this was an Axe Party zone, and knowing that he risked running into a campaign party, he realized he had to find some other clothes.

He peeked through the kei-apple hedge and saw a little homestead in the middle of the maize field. Laundry spread out on a line was swinging gently in the breeze. There seemed to be no one about.

He made a parting in the hedge and crept into the maize field, making his way cautiously towards the house, ready to spring to his feet and run should anyone raise alarm.

Ascertaining that there was indeed no one about, he tip-toed to the line and relieved it of one of the checked school shirts pegged there, slipping noiselessly back into the maize field.

Evening was setting in by the time he finally made his way to the road. He had skirted the shopping centre, making his way through the farms in a wide detour.

The trucks were no longer at the bushy homestead, neither was there any red shirt about. There was only the old man in the cane chair on the verandah beside a glowing jiko, his mangy dog curled up at his feet.

Yakobo flagged down a milk van, and for a fee, they agreed to drop him close to Chapa Kazi Farm, as they were headed that way.

It was pitch-dark when Yakobo finally got to the farm. He found everyone gathered at a huge bonfire JP had lit on the lawn next to the cattle *boma*, feasting.

"Where did you go off to?" said Juma, offering him a seat by the fire. "We have been worried about you."

"I lost my way," lied Juma, sighing and accepting a mug of hot soup from one of the lads. "I didn't know it would turn out that way." He felt the tender spot on his back where the tongue of a whip had licked him.

One of the youths, who was fingering the stolen loudhailer in his lap, probably figuring who among the video parlour owners in the township could have use for it, tossed the roach he had been smoking into the fire and said, "Eh, *Muthee*! In this kind of work you should expect anything!"

"Indeed you should," said another lad across, tenderly fingering a swelling lump on his brow.

"You should always know where your friends are too," added another, drinking from a chipped enamel mug. "You see for your case you strayed into enemy territory!" he said with a laugh, baring huge stained brown teeth.

There were huge pans filled with *githeri* and meat by the bonfire and Yakobo rose to help himself, for he realized he was real hungry, having had his last meal of porridge early that day.

JP emerged shortly from the main house, followed by the dark beefy man who had rode with him in the jeep, and whom the lads called Master.

"You did a real good job, my people," said JP, smiling at the faces around the fire. "That was real good of you. I thought you were going to be cowards when we got there, but how wrong I was!" he beamed, examining them with open pride. He seemed a little tipsy from the drinking that was going on in the main house where his wealthy friends were gathered. "You sure gave that Dove fellow a scare he will not forget in a hurry. I don't suppose he will be coming back to my ward any time soon!"

"We told you we were going to castrate him, *Mzee*," said the tall thin lad with brown teeth seated across from Yakobo. "*You* should know that we mean what we say!"

"Indeed! Let the fat dog attempt to organize another rally and he will see- I bet this time we'll go for his very balls...and hang them on a stick on the highway for the whole world to see!"

"No, I think we should put him in a sack and carry him off to Karura and keep him in an ant-bear hole until the elections are over!" supplied another youth across the fire, drawing sniggers.

"Indeed I believe you," said JP, laughing. "You truly are capable of anything."

"You know, *Mzee*, the fellow has yet to taste the bite of my *mathiokore* here," said a squat little fellow in a ill-fitting woolen coat, waving a hideous-looking heavy club fashioned out of a tree stump. "I made it especially for him!"

A round of laughter answered the midget's mock display of thrusting and clubbing at an imaginary cornered foe writhing on the ground.

There was five hundred shillings for each of them for their day's work, after which a drum of grain beer was brought from the store and they settled down to serious drinking.

It was in the small hours of the night when Yakobo, drunk as a tavern fly, finally stumbled off towards his house, mowing down the tall maize plants alongside the path as he staggered. Behind him Juma was no better for drink, his tall limbs sweeping in and out of each other's way like a circus marionette, a broken verse of a song the lads had composed in praise of JP and the Axe Party rolling off his slobbery lips in hiccupy lapses.

Back at the bonfire the youths, overcome by drink and weariness, gave up the hoarse singing and curled up in their coats on the ground in a snore. They were watched over by the fire, which occasionally sent a constellation of angry sparks spiraling heavenward as the night wind fanned the glowing embers.

Chapter Four

JP's winning speech was delivered at the same venue three weeks later. Contrary to what had been experienced at the market place when the Dove candidate had last been there this time a charged atmosphere of expectation and festivity hang over the little shopping centre.

A local band first drew and worked up the crowds of curious children hanging around the shops with popular *benga* tunes. They crowded around the huge dais, marveling at the powerful disco equipment and the fancy dress of the band. Some even tried to outdo the dancers on the stage, hitching up the long tails of their shirts and wriggling their puny bottoms at their riled friends. Slowly the elders started streaming in, abandoning their chores to find out what the hullabaloo was about. They were egged on by the announcement on the speakers mounted on the old truck doing the rounds in the village, and which was packed with youths clad in red t-shirts.

And so, when the jungle-green Range Rover drew up at the shopping centre and JP stepped out waving a walking stick, he was met with jubilation from the huge crowd that had gathered. He was immaculate in a flowing brightly-patterned *kitenge* shirt and ox-hide sandals, his Stetson resting at a trophy-hunter's angle on his head, carrying a carved ebony cane. Beside him was his wife Njeri, also brightly decked in waxed kitenge and an elaborate towering headscarf. Their son Gaitho was also with them, recently arrived from his studies in the US to help his father with the campaigns.

The reason for the crowd's excitement was partly because of the benefits the gathering had already brought them. The women ululated and ringed around the Range Rover, escorting it to the dais, strutting the new *khanga* clothes they had received, together with packets of *unga* and sugar. As for the men, they looked on from the sides, pleased all the same because they had some drinking money in their wallets. The kids were not left out either, gleefully fighting over biscuits and sweets scattered in the sand.

Yakobo stood at the fringe of all this activity, his eyes scanning the crowd nervously for trouble. He was still on edge after the scary experience they'd just had earlier at dawn with the Dove Party youths, who had mobbed them as they painted the wall dividing the Naivasha highway around the Sigona area red. A stationery truck had formed a barrier against oncoming traffic in the inside lane and Yakobo and a band of youth had sprang to the duty of pasting the Axe Party posters on the dangerous highway. That was until a truck of Dove youths had appeared from nowhere and it had been a scramble up the side of the moving truck as missiles flew dangerously above their heads.

Already Yakobo had enough scars from the campaign excursions of the days past; but such was the lure of it that once you were in, it was hard to pull out. And it was not just the money and free food and booze that came with the job. There was a certain thrill about going out there with the youths and kicking the opponent's ass.

One of the youths had however been injured in the dawn incident, hit by a speeding vehicle. The truck too had received quite a battering, a well-aimed rock shattering the windscreen. But they had survived.

JP mounted the dais and waved the walking stick at the crowd, and they roared back in a frenzy.

"*Asanteni*! Thank you!" he bellowed on the PA.

But just before he could launch into his speech his aide, the dark ever- scowling Master walked up and presented him his cell phone. He spoke briefly into the phone, his moist face lighting up, before handing it back to Master.

Soon after there was a commotion at the back of the gathering. People were running towards the main road, where something had been sighted.

Slowly a convoy of expensive vehicles made their way through the crowd, their headlights burning, horns blaring, making for the dais. A band of youths in red shirts quickly threw a cordon around the vehicles, clearing a narrow passage in the crowd that snaked up to the spot where JP had parked his Range Rover. The roof of one of the high four-wheel-drive vehicles slid open and a fat light-skinned man with a shiny baldhead stood up, waving a flywhisk at the crowd. It was none other than the presidential candidate of the Axe Party!

The frenzy that followed proved tricky, the youths finding it hard to contain the crowds. The new arrivals had come with their own drumming party and a long party of singing dancers waving placards and blowing whistles and trumpets. It was like a war party.

All activity at the little shopping centre, that had initially been the preserve of the Dove Party candidate, was brought to a halt. The peasants on the farms neighbouring the town abandoned their work and flocked to the market, drawn by the noise.

With difficulty the youths managed to get the new arrivals out of their vehicles and elbow a way for them up to the dais, ushering them to their seats lined up at the front. JP was at hand to welcome them with a hug and a kiss for the ladies.

"Alright, *Asanteni, wananchi!*" said JP, walking up to the battery of microphones, waving at the crowds to calm down. At the far end of the dais his son Gaitho panned in with his camcorder, recording the lively event. TV cameramen who had accompanied the convoy also raced from their vans, hurriedly setting up their equipment on tripods to capture the campaign for the evening news. Within a short while the market place was packed to the brim, with part of the crowd scrambling up the rusty zinc roofs and others perching up trees to get a birds' eye view.

"*Asanteni! Asanteni!*" bellowed JP, waving frantically. "Thank you so much for the princely welcome, people of Gachie! I think if I say we are already in Parliament I won't be lying, or will I?" he paused, cocking his ear at the crowd, which roared back in assent.

"Indeed, I can't be lying; not in front of all these people. The Axe Party is indeed not just in Parliament, but in State House as well!" he swept around to glance at the presidential candidate. "*Bwana Mheshimiwa*, these people you see here are telling you only one thing, they are taking you to State House!"

A roar of applause interrupted him, drowning the words on the PA.

"Yes, the Axe has come to Gachie to hack down the tree where the worthless dove was nesting, the tree of domination and oppression that has stood in your midst for so long. The tree that has kept you in the shade and blocked the light from reaching you all these years- we have come to cut it down! And it is you and your vote who have honed the axe into the razor-sharp weapon it has become today... I tell you, this is truly the dawn of a new era, and no one dare stand in the way of the axe...!" said JP, quite in his element before the bank of microphones and the frenzied crowd. "And just to prove that this is not empty talk, let our guests here hear for themselves what the axe will do...People,... one, two, three... SHOKAAA...!"

"*Kata...Chinjaaa...!*" roared the crowd in response to the party's campaign slogan, led by the strategically placed groups of hecklers.

"Aha!" said JP, satisfied. "Indeed that is just what the axe will do to the dove's nesting tree! And I want any Dove moles in this gathering to take the word to those cowards! ...Heh? It is no secret, is it?" he paused at the hushed crowd. "I know that their informers are here alright, hiding amongst you my people, watching to see what will happen here. They are scared stiff... those cowards, long before the day of the actual voting comes,...Ha-ha-haaaa...!" He took out a handkerchief and wiped his brow.

"The Axe Party, my people, is here to bring light to this area," resumed JP after the applause had died down, punctuating his sentences with a wave of his carved walking stick at the audience. "And we are not just saying this, but we mean every word. We want to bring the people of this area food; we bring you good roads to take the produce of your farms to market in Nairobi; we bring you education for your children; we bring you jobs for your youth; we bring you electricity to light your homes; we bring you piped water to run in your kitchens; we bring you...development! We bring you l-i-g-h-t...!"

The restraining beacons that the organizing youth had installed around the dais to keep back the crowds snapped like matchsticks as the crowd surged forward. It soon became such that all the Party youth stationed around the shops had to hurriedly convene around the dais and reinforce the cordon, shoving back the crowds. It was going to be a long, sweaty day.

***

A weeklong period of festivity followed the elections, in which hundreds of people flocked to the farm to celebrate, all filing to the huge marquee tent pitched on the lawn in front of the farmhouse where all the activity was. Huge charcoal cauldrons had been brought from the nearby school and set up in a corner of the lawn, and inside boiled *githeri* and bone soup all day round.

The hired school cooks wrestled with the giant pestles as they turned the *ugali* above the wood fires, sweat trickling down their faces and off their chins in runnels down their bared bellies. As they paused to wipe themselves with soiled handkerchiefs droplets of the sweat inescapably fell into the giant pans. But that was not to matter. The food was still tasty, all the same.

The *wananchi* made a beeline for the serving table and had their plastic plates piled high with grain, bone and soup. And then, smiling, they went to find a place to sit in the tent or on the lawns.

In the backyard the wealthy man's dogs growled over the boiled heads of the five bulls that had been slaughtered.

Amidst all this activity JP and his wife moved, stopping to chat up the feasting people, tasting a piece of meat here, or sipping some soup there.

Sometimes they joined the drummers in the little tent erected beside the giant marquee where grain beer was served from giant drums.

Whenever JP was sighted the dancers would create a path and herd him into the circle, where the best dancers would quickly crowd him, their oiled limbs and waists gyrating, seasoned tongues parroting his praises up to the ridges yonder.

At this point the tempo of the drumming would gradually rise and JP was left with little option but to sway into the clutches of the dancer and shake a leg.

And then, on the fifth day of the week the gates of Chapa Kazi farm were drawn shut and the revelers, on turning up, found that the Maasai guards had resumed their no-nonsense look. It was over as abruptly as it had started.

Chapter Five

YAKOBO'S promotion came in the form of his being taken to work in the cattle *boma*. Following JP's election victory Yakobo found that the wealthy man and his wife gradually took him more into their wing.

Often he would be called upon to accompany Juma and the boss in the old jeep to the nearby town to purchase farm supplies. Sometimes he was sent with a driver to deliver cabbages and green maize to the local school or to other customers in the neighbourhood who ordered from the farm. These errands were enjoyable because they would be spared the backbreaking monotony that was working the long coffee lines in the blazing sun. Also often there was the likelihood they would remain with a surplus that they hadn't sold at the end of the day. At such times, JP or his wife would regard the little mound of cabbages and, seeing they were going into their third day, would invite them to take their pick and deliver the rest to the kitchen to make the following day's broth. This was the same for the milk that they couldn't sell.

Such were the benefits of working in the *boma* Yakobo would hardly go home empty-handed at the end of the day.

But perhaps even greater than the new benefits of his new posting was the birth of his daughter, Mukami.

It had been amazing how Njambi had carried the pregnancy, quite unlike what had been the case with Ndonga. The woman had gone out to work the farm as usual, lugging sacks of coffee beans or weeding the rows of the young crop further down by the riverbank. Seeing her busy at work, her *lesso* cloth secured around her waist, Yakobo had hardly remembered that she was indeed with child. That is until an excited Juma had fetched him one day from the nappier field, dragging him by the hand, refusing to divulge the cause for the urgency and excitement until they were upon the scene.

She had gone into labour halfway down one of the long lines she had been weeding, collapsing with a gasp underneath a coffee bush. On hearing the cry, the other women had abandoned their work and crowded around her, throwing a screen of *lessos* to keep out prying eyes. It had been an easy delivery, taking less than ten minutes, after which the women broke out in ululations, thanking the creator for the gift, as they gaped at the little one wrapped up in pieces of old clothes.

This time Yakobo had a fat fowl slaughtered for the newborn, and as the old midwife from Kampi Nyasi attended to the overjoyed Njambi, he left to find Juma so that they could go celebrate with a drink down at Mama Pima's. For it was double blessings for him, and it was worthy celebrating.

"You really have made me envious this time around, my friend," said Juma, sipping from the glass. "First the boy, and now you have a little girl; just the perfect family anyone would dream of! I daresay you have made me reflect quite a bit on my own life. I really think I should find a woman and marry now, my friend."

"Oh, is that Juma speaking, or are my ears hearing wrong?" called the liquor-seller from the shadows close to the fireplace. "Juma, of all people, you say you want to marry? I'd say you forget it. Not when you continue having it easy with the women of Kampi Nyasi, you won't!"

There were guffaws all around the table at the woman's statement.

The little hut was smoky and crowded, the grimy farmhands squeezed on the two benches in the sitting area holding their drinks, eyes watery in the semi-dark. They were mostly the regular fellows from Kampi Nyasi, although there were a few from the neighbouring farms, some trekking all the way from as far as Ndenderu to drink because the potency of Mama Pima's stuff was known far and wide.

"So you think I don't have the tongue to talk someone's daughter into shacking up with me to start a family, is that what you are saying?" said Juma, piqued.

"Honestly, I don't see it happening while we are still in this Kampi Nyasi," replied the brewer.

"And why not? Is he not man enough?" supplied someone from the dark corner.

"Not quite," said Mama Pima, emerging to take an order, holding a stained plastic bottle half-full of liquor and a tiny measuring glass. She was a fat dark woman with a voluminous bust and thick stout legs that gave her the air of an immovable midget, and whose muscular hands were well adapted to the task of throwing out drunks who became a nuisance in the place. She had a squinted gaze, her beady bright eyes hooded by thinning brows, but which were nevertheless alert. The sort of eyes the patrons said were set on the drinker's purse, trained on their hard-earned silver like a chameleon to a fly.

"What I meant is that the women of this Kampi Nyasi are not going to allow it. Not when they have him tight in their grasp like *smaku* and paper."

There were drunken guffaws all around.

It was getting steadily dark. More customers streamed into the place, causing a sitting crisis because all the benches were occupied.

Mama Pima went to the hearth to light a tin-lamp, which she brought to the table, examining the contents of everyone's glass.

"You, Njenga, you have been nursing that five-shilling measure all evening. Come on, drain it and give back the glass!" she glared at an old man snuggled comfortably in the corner. "You are not going to cause my faithful customers to drink while standing for such a miserly measure of drink...come on, drink it up!"

"Did you hear that? The woman has sniffed the smell of money now," quipped a drunk from the shadows.

"Hey, but this is still liquor," protested Njenga's friend seated across. "Five shillings or a shilling, I say the man still bought it with his money; and so he has a right to enjoy it any way he wants!"

There was a murmur of agreement from around the table. As for the assailed man, he sat stolidly by, gripping the near-empty glass tightly, making no move to toss back the slug. "Your moneyed customers can sit there on the bed, for all I care," he said coolly, smacking his wet trembly red lips that were peeling from too much hard drinking. "This is a public house, and I got every right to come and go as I please."

"*He-he-heee...!*" laughed another drunk in the dancing shadows. "Tell her, Njenga. Doesn't she know that this is a *kilabu*?"

"Look, I won't have any of you sitting on my bed," said Mama Pima to the two new arrivals, and who, on Njenga's prompting, were heading for the old bed by the wall, and which was screened from the sitting area by an old bed sheet.

"And why shouldn't they?" said Juma with mock surprise.

"Why shouldn't they?" Mama Pima's round face creased into fat black caterpillars at the brow when she scowled. "You've got to be my husband to sit on that bed, that's why," she said, stabbing a fat little finger in Juma's face.

"Aha, I see. But then, all these years I've been drinking here I've never seen the poor man's face!"

"Ho-ho-hoooo...!" laughed the drunk in the corner, his eyes glistening with tears. "You are right. I am yet to see the man of this house too."

"She might as well pick any of these young men here to do the honours...I mean; it's not exactly a crime."

"Mind what you speak, young man!" snarled the thickset woman, wagging a stubby finger under his nose.

"See?" said Njenga, smarting from a doze. "The woman has grown so rich from the men of Kampi Nyasi she now has the audacity to hurl abuse at them, forgetting they were the ones who welcomed her here."

"Njenga, what did you say?" fumed Mama Pima, standing on the balls of her flat little feet, ready to lunge across the table.

"I say you don't cheat me, woman," said the old man, his trembly index finger pointed, unwavering in her knit-browed glare. "Don't you think that because my hair goes to grey my mind does the same. I remember very well the day you came to Kampi Nyasi, you Mama Pima. You were a scroungy little thing that no self-respecting man would look at twice, I saw you with my very eyes."

In the ensuing drunken laughter the brewer cursed and glared, her face twitching angrily. But Juma restrained her.

"Come on, find the visitors some place to sit, mama. You know you cannot win a war of words against a drunk. In any case, I don't think Njenga is ready to leave just yet. At least not when he still has the stomach for one more drink."

"Ha! Ha! You are right my friend," said the grey-haired old man, reaching a bony hand across to shake Juma's hand. "And I have the money too, or don't I?" He reached into his inside coat pocket and took out a five-shilling coin, which he tossed triumphantly on the table after close examination to ascertain it was not something bigger. "I say, bring the drink, woman! Today we must finish the whole of your stock, for aren't we celebrating Yakobo's little girl? Here, brother, I don't have *ukimwi* you know. You can have a sip from my glass here- if only for the baby!"

Yakobo accepted the glass and raised it to his mouth before returning it. And then he placed in an order for a whole 'jik' bottle for the entire table.

"See? I told you!" said Njenga, exalted at so much to drink. "Yakobo's hand has always been an open one. He is a true wa-Nyumba indeed!"

"True word," supplied someone at the other end of the table, tongue in cheek. "The brother has an open hand indeed. And it seems like there are quite a number of us who were waiting here all evening for just such a godsend!"

And as the drunks sung Yakobo's praises to the distant ridges and settled down to do justice to his order, Mama Pima was left with little option but to go out and borrow stools from her neighbours to accommodate the full house.

It was in the wee hours of the night when they finally staggered through the maize field home to bed, their songs of merriment disturbing the peace of the night.

It was going to be a struggle for Njambi to wake Yakobo early the following morning to milk the cows. For that one moment, life was sheer joy.

Chapter Six

NDONGA was a little impatient with his little sister Mukami. He didn't understand why it took her so long to learn to walk. Such a simple thing as putting one foot in front of the other and swinging your hands, and yet it had to take days for her to muster!

Their father sat on the folding chair outside the house watching them play underneath the gnarled little tree. Yakobo was feeling a little unwell, and had begged leave off work that day. Juma had had to find someone else from the farm to stand in for him.

It had appeared like a mild case of fever the evening before, and which he had hoped would wear off with a good night's sleep. But as the night progressed, it had not just got serious, but the coughing had come back in earnest too, the warm air resounding in his chest like a gust of gritty wind whistling through a rocky cavern. He had been forced to send his wife to inform JP early at dawn before she had gone off to the coffee estate.

As he watched his children play, enjoying the warm feel of the morning sun on the back of his head, he hoped the aspirins JP's wife had given him would lessen the fever enough by evening so that he could milk the cows. He was short of cash, and needed the half bottle measure that came with the job for the children's tea.

Watching the boy, it was amazing how tall he had grown. It was only the other day when he was born. And yet, now that he reflected back, he realized that they had indeed been four years on the farm. It seemed like only yesterday when they had put up the house, and the other day when they had done the campaign for JP!

"Hey, careful there!" Yakobo turned to shout a caution at the boy. "Use the stick, will you? Why do you have such a strong head?" Ndonga, growing impatient, had abandoned the stick that he had been using to lead his sister and was now trying to get her to stay upright by holding her up by the armpits and egging her on with his knees. He derived a lot of amusement in the frightened look that came on her face every time he let go. As she clawed at the air, wobbling unsteadily on her feet, he would race round to the front and make faces at her as he rolled on the ground with laughter.

"Keep to the stick, Ndonga, hear? You won't teach your sister to walk that way- you are only making her scared!"

"*Eee...*Baba!" said the boy, helping his sister to her feet. He paused to wipe the snot trickling from his nose with the back of his hand, drying it on the torn seat of his pants, before taking up the stick.

He was a naughty one, this Ndonga. Always in a hurry to sneak away to the cherry factory down by the river where he liked to sit with the factory hands and play ball with his friends from Kampi Nyasi. Lately he had been getting into a lot of mischief down in the village where they went to scavenge for old tins to make toy cars with. Just the other day Mama Pima had reported seeing him and two other boys outside the off-license pub someone had opened down the street to sell bottled beer. That they had been pretending to scavenge for bottle tops on the nearby garbage heap. But really all they were waiting for was for the wind to lift the lace curtain in the entranceway so that they could steal a peek at the action inside, where the patrons were dancing to the blaring jukebox. On seeing her, they had promptly taken off into the alleys.

Yakobo was uneasy with all the reports he kept receiving about the boy, together with the company he kept. It was easy to imagine what a gang of boys with a few coins from their labour on the farm could get up to. And yet Kampi Nyasi had been getting even more crowded lately as the estate grew steadily into the hills to the west of the farm.

Perhaps it was time he thought of sending the boy away to school somewhere. Yes, at his age he should be eligible to nursery class. Indeed it was time for the boy to get a little education, if only to keep him out of mischief while they were away at work.

But then, come to think of it, there really was no school anywhere in Kampi Nyasi that he knew of. It was strange, but there was hardly any school anywhere in the neighbourhood that he could take the boy to. The closest one he knew was two miles away in Kiringari; and they didn't admit penniless boys from the farmlands. It was a school for the rich farm-owners' children.

There was that long thatched block in Kampi Nyasi that had once served the purpose. But it had long since transformed into a lodging house for a bunch of young unmarried men after the few pupils one by one left to join their parents picking coffee on the estate, or migrated to other estates. Some of the parents had even forcibly withdrawn their children, arguing that they needed to help bring in the *ugali* on the family table with the worsening hard times.

That had been a whole two years back, and since then no one had made an attempt to revive the venture. The headmaster had long left Kampi Nyasi to work in a neighbouring township, same to his few staff.

Perhaps it was time Yakobo mooted the idea of

restarting the school with those parents who had school-age children.

And as Yakobo reminisced, he paused to cup his hand over his mouth as a bout of coughing seized him. He clasped at his paining chest as he hawked, trying to clear the tightness in his lungs. He worked up a thick blob of yellow sputum and shot it into the dust, rubbing it in with his heel.

When the coughing passed he reached for the tub of water at his feet and drank, squinting his eyes because it was getting increasingly difficult to swallow. Even plain water traveled with excruciating pain down his inflamed throat. He wondered what sort of cough this could be.

Far at the other end of the yard the boy was leading his sister deeper into the maize field, goading her on by lowering the smooth green stems across her way. He pushed the stem further out of her grasp every time she neared it, cackling with laughter at her cries of protest.

***

It rained heavily that evening after Njambi had come back from the coffee fields.

The late season rains poured out of nowhere, drenching the country and soaking into the thirsty earth. It was amazing because the clear skies of the rest of the day had hardly hinted at it. That is until late afternoon when it had suddenly darkened, a thick grey cloud spreading across the sky from the direction of Limuru. And then, just like that the heavy rain drops had started pelting the dusty thatches of Kampi Nyasi, hardly giving the villagers time enough to gather the children's urine-soaked bedding rags which they had put out to dry on the roofs. Such rains as those who knew the weather well knew wouldn't last long.

Yakobo had just returned from milking the cows, assisted by Ndonga, who carried the pail for him from one cage to the next and kept the cows replenished with salt lick and feed as they were milked. It had taken him longer because of the waning signs of the fever and the pain he still felt in his chest every time he bent down. But he had completed without hitch.

It was as they sat around the little *jiko* Njambi had filled with glowing coals, warming after the herbal bath she had prepared for him that the rain started.

It drove against the slapdash iron roof in a steady patter for a brief moment, and then retreated to recollect.

"Ah, that certainly is a good sign," said Yakobo, straightening his hands over the glowing coals. He creened his neck to look out at the distant grey-streaked line of hills through the partly open door. He was hardly surprised, especially after the huge grey clouds had suddenly gathered in the sky. Ndonga reached into his shorts pocket and produced a cob of green maize he had stolen from someone's field earlier in the day, eyeing it surreptitiously in the shadow cast by his folded knee. Certain that no one had seen him he pushed it into the ashes in the little compartment underneath the coals. He then sat squatted on the floor, watching it intently as it slowly changed a golden brown.

"It is a blessing indeed for the vegetables," said Njambi, stuffing ash into a punctured tin to make lye. On her lap Mukami suckled heartily at her sagging breast, oblivious of her mother's remonstrations.

"Ah! Don't *bite*, you little scoundrel!" said Njambi, slapping her lightly on the cheek. "Can't you suckle like other children? In any case, the breast is all yours, so what's the hurry?"

Ndonga, now lying on his belly with his chin resting on an ashy palm, sucked at his thumb and laughed. "She is very greedy, this *Toto*," he quipped.

"*Eeei*! Watch your tongue, you other bigmouth! As if you were any better yourself," said their mother, eyeing Ndonga. "Still, maybe it's time I stopped suckling your sister here. She has grown into a big girl now, old enough to eat *githeri* and porridge."

"Yes, you should do that, Mama. She is old enough top eat hard *githeri* like everyone else, and not to be pampered around all the time like a queen termite."

"And you," she turned her rage on Ndonga, "will you stop laughing like a fool and rise off that floor? Look at you, all covered in ashes, and yet I bathed you just now!"

"And pull that thumb out of your mouth too," said Yakobo as he accepted a mug of millet porridge from his wife. "At your age you should have stopped that long ago."

But the boy only gave them the benefit of his gap-toothed smile, flashing the inflamed red gum where his mother had forcibly removed a loose tooth just the other day, and went about his business unperturbed.

"I wonder where he got the cob he is roasting from," said Yakobo, sipping from the steaming mug. "The maize on the farm is hardly ready."

"Probably stole it from someone's farm down by the river," supplied Njambi, eyeing him scornfully. "This boy is turning into a rogue, I tell you- him together with the other boys he roams the alleys of Kampi Nyasi with the whole day. You must start cracking your whip on him, I tell you!"

But their conversation was interrupted by the renewed downpour that hammered even more thunderously on the weak roof, the accompanying hailstones threatening to tear right through the rusty zinc.

"*Ooi!* Speak of the devil!" said Njambi, gazing fearfully at the rattling roof. "So when we praised it it went back to bring out its harnessed wrath!"

For a whole ten minutes the rain and hail beat steadily down, a frozen moment in which only the tin lamp on the table flickered in the darkening hut as the family listened to the thundering forces of nature.

And then the hail abated and with it the fury, leaving a weak drizzle that pattered lightly on the overlapping scraps of flattened metal. Already leaks had started in several places in the roof, and Njambi had to dash around positioning pans and tins underneath the trickle to collect the water.

It was as Yakobo was observing a more serious leak that had started at a spot in the apex above where they slept that they heard someone call outside.

He buttoned up his coat and went to open the door, thinking it was Joshua coming round to check on his health, and probably see if they could go down to Mama Pima's after the rain abated.

But it turned out to be one of the Maasai guards, who stood leaning on his long white stick. He had been sent by JP to fetch him to see to an emergency in the cattle yard. Apparently one of the expectant heifers had commenced labour.

Alarmed, Yakobo collected his straw hat hanging from a nail on the sooty rafters and left.

But then, Ndonga was not to be left behind. He grabbed his half-cooked cob from the hot ashes and raced out after his father, barely stopping long enough to don a torn old sweater his mother had pulled from a pile of clothing on the bed.

In the ensuing silence in the hut after they had left the rain pattered softly on the roof, dripping down the eave into the uneven gutter along the raised earth verge embracing the rotting walls, ...ta, ta, ta! ...ta, ta, ta!...

Slowly pools of soot-coloured water collected in the containers she had distributed around to receive the leak from the roof, the surface ringing with ripples every time an additional drop fell.

And in the cozy warmth around the glowing fire Mukami, fed and suckled, soon curled up in her mother's lap and, with her hand still buried in the folds of her dress next to the warm breast, she fell asleep.

Njambi lifted the child and put her to sleep on their narrow bed, covering her with an old blanket.

As she moved back to the hearth to start popping the peas out of their pods for the evening meal, she stopped. A dark figure loomed in the doorway, the door having been pushed inward soundlessly.

"I too would easily fall asleep beside a warm fire in this lousy weather," said JP, stepping into the hut and pushing the door half shut behind him. He was laughing softly. "Especially so in the arms of a pretty caring woman like you, Mama Ndonga."

There was a sinister smile on his face as he advanced towards her. Stopping an arm's reach away, he took off his wet Stetson and twirled it slowly between his fingers in a manner that seemed habitual to him, kneading the soaked leather thoughtfully. The padding in the long leather coat he wore, this close, made his shoulders appear even bigger, his presence domineering.

"The day has died, *Mzee*," said Njambi, barely masking the surprise in her voice. "Can I offer you something?" She took a step back, moving towards the hearth.

She hoped her nervousness didn't show, for as she looked into the man's eyes she sensed somehow that he hadn't come on an ordinary inspection call.

"Hmmm...I'd like to ...indeed I would enjoy it, waYakobo," he said in a strange soft voice, looking casually around him. "*Ei!* This rain has drenched me to the bone- thank God your house was close by. Otherwise I would be thoroughly soaked by the time I got to the house. Indeed I wouldn't mind something warm to warm me up a little, waYakobo."

"I hope we have something in the pots to offer. There is a seat over there, *Mzee*." She approached the pot by the hearth, her eyes darting from the standing visitor to the child sleeping on the bed. In the silence that had engulfed the room the drizzle pattered on on the old roof. In the cold breeze from the partly open door the light of the lamp danced left and right, casting his looming figure in silhouette.

"The children have grown up quite," said JP in the same testy voice, looking towards the bed, still standing despite the seat offered him.

Njambi nodded, following his gaze nervously.

"The boy, how old is he now?"

"Four years. Going to five."

"I see," he said, nodding, still twirling the hat slowly round and round. In the yellow light of the tin lamp the thick gold wedding band on his finger glinted. "Such a fine lad he is too. Perhaps it is time he got some schooling?" he said, as if on the spur of the moment. Nevertheless the words were laced with suggestive innuendo.

"School...yes, *Mzee*. We think about it," said Njambi, now rather nervous. "His father and I think about it a lot." She couldn't herald the object of the questioning. She wished Yakobo would return soon. Somehow, she didn't feel comfortable alone with her employer in the hut.

"Aha! But then, where would you take him? There is no school around here that I can think of...that is, other than the mission school in Kiringari. They say the children there are put on very good discipline, and they pass their exams quite well. It might just be the ideal school to take a child to. My driver passes that way delivering milk every morning."

Njambi was quiet, not knowing how to respond.

"Yes, it is just the ideal school for the boy," said JP, nodding. "You must give thought to sending him there. It is not good for such a fine lad to lack an education."

"It is a good idea," she said simply, wondering what the man was driving at.

"Kiringari is a very good school. I personally know the Headmaster. I would ensure he gives the boy utmost attention."

Njambi was quiet, her gaze trained at the floor. As they were speaking the patter of the drizzle on the roof increased, and soon the rain was pissing down, the accompanying misty spray driving into the doorway, wetting the beat floor. He turned and pushed the door shut. Then he walked slowly towards her, his eyes, which were now fixed on her, darkening.

"Njambi, come closer here, I want to ask you something," he said, gesturing with a finger.

"Why?" she said, mystified at the change in him.

"I can't hear you very well with the noise," he said, gesturing at the roof.

She remained rooted to the spot, albeit now her breathing quickening.

He advanced slowly until he stood nose to nose with her, the blazing log fire in the hearth casting his face in fiery profile.

"Njambi, you know you are a very beautiful woman," he said suddenly, his voice turned husky, studying the curve of her chin and the line of her neck down to her bust, which was still partly unbuttoned from suckling the child.

"Yes, very beautiful," he said again, licking his lips nervously. "Does Yakobo ever tell you that?"

Njambi was still, her thoughts racing, chest heaving. In the noise of the downpour she could hear her own heart throb in her chest.

"*Ohooo...*I see he doesn't," there was a bright gleam in his eye, his lips, that were wet with slobber, quivering as if with a little uncertainty. "Well, the man is a fool if he doesn't see it. You are truly a beautiful woman, Mama Ndonga." He was close enough so she could feel his warm breath on her skin. "Tell you what," he said in a whisper, bending his head to one side so he could gaze deeper into her down turned eyes. "We can even make each other happy, you and I, you know, Mama Ndonga... Just the two of us. Yes, we can be very happy together, you know." He was staring deep into her eyes, his face gone moist in the excitement building inside. His lips curled upwards slowly in a half smile, just as he raised a hand to touch her cheek.

"*Don't!*" hissed Njambi suddenly, stepping back. "What are these things you say, *Mzee*?" There was fright in her eyes, which had gone wide with disbelief. In her breast her heart was palpitating wildly. "You

know I am Yakobo's woman, *Mzee*, and you can't..."
she was unable to complete the sentence, the word too
heavy on her slack jaw.

JP watched her in silence for a while, his hand
held awkwardly by his side.

Just at that moment Yakobo's voice was heard
outside, calling on the boy to hurry on. They were
returning from the cattle *boma*.

"Aaah!" said JP, stepping back. In the dim light of
the lamp a dark shadow passed over his moist face.

Putting the hat back on his head, the farm-owner
cast the woman one last look, which was loaded with
indiscernible intent, and turned and ducked out into
the rain, slipping noiselessly into the darkness.

Chapter Seven

JUMA was sent to fetch Ndonga early the following morning.

The boy, startled out of sleep, hurriedly slurped down his salty porridge that had weevil carapaces floating in it and went outside, followed shortly after by his mother, the little girl strapped to her back. It was still early, birds calling all over the lightening country, which hang thick with mist following the heavy downpour of the evening before.

They found JP standing outside the tool shed, watching the farmhands as they collected their work tools and left. As Njambi went in to collect her tin and sisal bag she noticed a similar sack and tin on the ground at the farm-owner's feet.

"Come here, *kijana*," said JP to the boy, signaling with a finger. Ndonga, still puzzled about the summoning, detached himself from his mother and ran up to the farm-owner, his frightened gaze trained on the ground. He was certain he had done nothing wrong the day before ...or had he? He had only gone down to the cherry store in the afternoon as usual after his sister had dozed off in the shade. He remembered only playing ball with his friends in the field behind the store. They hadn't ventured into Kampi Nyasi at all, neither had they gone for a swim in the river. And so, what could the matter be?

"Take those," said JP pointing at the tin and sack. Then, with a cursory glance at his shiny watch, "I expect that bag filled by the end of the day. It's time you stopped idling around and started earning your keep on the farm."

Yakobo, who had been pushing a barrow-load of manure scrapped from the cattle pen, his second job of the day after milking the cows, stopped and leaned against the thick barrow handles, watching his son join the other women and children as they filed off through the maize field.

Thinking it was his wife's idea that their son join the workforce, he was about to hurry after them and stop him when, looking towards the tool shed, he saw JP coming his way, swinging his carved walking stick. Yakobo took up the barrow handles and gave a heave, propelling it through the syrupy mud.

"Working real hard, are you now?" said JP when he returned from the nearby manure heap. He was standing in the concreted feeding yard beside the rusty troughs that had been fashioned out of old oil drums sliced through the middle from top to bottom with a hacksaw, and which were mounted on stout wooden stands. The look on JP's face was not pleasant. He seemed rather agitated. "Good work, eh?" he said, surveying the muddy yard with slitted eyes.

"Er, good day, *Mzee*," said Yakobo nervously, standing to attention beside the dung-creased wheelbarrow, not certain whether to go on into the yard.

JP turned and examined the cows lined up in the cages behind him, watching the two of them with their liquid black eyes, some mooing softly in anticipation of their feed.

"Yakobo, you are starting to become careless with the work," he said, poking at a scab of dried dung plastered on the concrete with the tip of his cane. "You don't scrub and hose down this place often enough, do you?"

"Er...*Mzee*..."

"Yes, go on and lie to me," he said, watching him calmly from underneath his hooded eyebrows. "You know very well that *Mzee* is busy attending to office matters these days, and so you can well sit around and do the work as you please, isn't it? Look at this!" He walked over to the watering trough and drew a line with the tip of the cane through the crusting muddy sediment at the bottom, causing grains of earth to disturb the clarity of the rainwater that had collected inside. "You scrub down the place regularly, is that what you want to tell me?" He eyed the dumbstruck farm hand for a while, his beady eyes laced with loathing. Then he walked over to the post and rail fence hemming in the cement yard and stood with his forearms resting on the top rail, looking out into the grassless yard that the cows had trampled into squelchy dung-coloured mush as they exercised. He looked at the crush at the far end of the yard, which had one of the rails hanging loose where a cow had kicked it as Yakobo struggled to push a bottle of deworming concentrate down its throat the week before.

"You are becoming real careless, Yakobo," said JP, nodding slowly.

He walked slowly down the concrete yard, peering in at the cows; his little nose puckering at the strong ammoniac fumes of the urine the cows had pissed in the night, and which Yakobo was yet to clean out of the blocked drain at the back of the row of cages.

Yakobo walked slowly by, his hands clasped behind his back, head hung, awaiting the worst from his boss. And it was a mistake of his own making too. The past four days he had not scrubbed the place well at all, owing to the fever, that ate into his joints when it peaked such that it was impossible to hold anything firmly. And yet, for some reason Yakobo refused to admit even to himself that it was getting serious, willing it to go away, afraid of telling his boss. He knew what they would do. JP would take him to the mission hospital in Kikuyu, where the sisters would insist on admitting him into the ward after examining his chest. And as they kept him there, pampering him with expensive hospital food, the bill would grow and grow. At the end of it they would probably dismiss him with a warning to lay off arduous manual work.

This picture was clear enough in his mind because it was just a few years back when he had had to steal his way from the same hospital disguised in an old coat Njambi had smuggled in and gone back to his spray job on the flower farm. He remembered clearly what the sister with a thin long face had said to him at the time, looking at the x-ray picture, staring at him down her long hooked noise as he lay there on the starched white sheets. That his chest was rotted by spray chemicals inhaled over years working on the farm.

Well, he was damned if he was going to walk himself in there a second time. Didn't these people know he had a family to care for?

It was with a feeling of relief that he watched JP finally walk out of the yard after a lengthy admonition that Yakobo had taken in silence, head bowed. At the end he had mumbled a dozen apologies and pleaded, short of kneeling at his feet, to be given another chance to make up the mess.

With JP gone, he set about scrubbing the yard with the stiff wire broom, flooding it with water from the hose. And as he jerked on the long broom handle he felt the pain shoot like needles inside his wrist and elbow joints, causing beads of sweat to spring to his brow. He bit his lower lip and worked even more furiously, fighting the fever with his whole heart, even as the pungent sweat drenched him all over, causing his nylon shirt to plaster to his back underneath his worn coat. He had a few aspirin tablets that his wife had brought him from the village inside his hip pocket. He would take them later in the day as the sun rose higher in the sky.

Over at the coffee estate, Ndonga, allocated a line by Juma, set about the tricky task of filling his tin with the ripe red berries. The berries were not in shortage, for the leafy branches hang thick with them at that time of year, luscious and red, giving way easily on touch. The problem was accessing the higher branches where most of them were. It meant he had to clamber up the tree, his tin carefully balanced in one hand to avoid spilling what he had already collected. The chill inside the bushy estate at that early hour made matters no easier.

He could see a few of his friends among the busy workers. However, they had been allocated lines far from his and after a few attempts at shouted conversation, they had to give it up and instead concentrate on filling their sacks. His mother too had been taken to work further up the slope. Now it remained only for one to struggle with the hanging leafy bushes, dodging the dew that shook out of the leaves, which had by them wetted his face and the front of his shirt.

Soon Ndonga had scratches all over on his exposed thighs and shins from clambering up the trees, which itched when the dew ran in them. And yet he couldn't stop to scratch himself and wipe his face. Already he was drawing the tail as the more experienced pickers made their way easily up the lines.

It was as he was returning a while later from emptying his first tin-full in the sack that a cry rent the lush hillside buzzing with foraging humanity.

Everyone abandoned their tasks momentarily to see what the matter was.

It turned out to be one of the boys who had disturbed a nest of wasps up a bush he had been working on, and who had been stung senseless for his effort. As the whimpering boy was led off to the little office by the cherry store, snot and tears running down his already swelling face, the pickers returned to their lines. It was only one of the momentary distractions that characterized the seemingly endless foraging up the long winding lines that was the order of the day on the vast estate.

And yet every moment on the job counted. The bespectacled old cashier seated behind the old till in the grilled window at the little office down by the factory paid out the two twenty-shilling coins only to the worker who had attained a full sack measure. And there was no fooling him because he trusted only what the weighing scales told him. Anything short was presumed a wasted day, for which nothing would be paid, even as the beans were poured down the spout into the pit, where they were sucked on into the belly of the clanging hulling machine. All that after the laborious sorting in the collection yard, where the green beans were separated to be dried into '*mbuni*', further reducing the measure. For, at the end of it all, they were still JP's produce, or weren't they?

Chapter Eight

WHEN the weary Njambi and her son returned from the weighing centre down by the river, they found Yakobo stretched out on the bed, covered up to the chin with the thin patched blanket. The little girl, unattended since earlier at noon when she had been left with her father, sat on the floor playing with a huge bug that was flailing its legs helplessly, unable to get off its back. She was poking repeatedly at it with a stick, breaking into a triumphant four-toothed smile every time it clasped the end of the stick. Mukami was covered all over in ashes and dirt from her rounds of mischief around the house.

"Yakobo?" called Njambi, approaching the bed, a note of fear creeping into her voice. It was dark inside the house with the fast falling dusk. "Are you alright?"

He stared back at her, his eyes, huge shiny white balls, narrowing slightly in the gloom as he registered her presence.

"Have you milked the cows?"

Still there was no answer.

Alarmed, she reached out a trembly hand and touched his brow. He was running an alarmingly high temperature, and yet he was shivering with obvious cold underneath the blanket, which he clutched tightly about him as if it had the power to ward off the fever.

She traced her callused hand tenderly down the side of his face, feeling his jaw, which was locked tightly, teeth clenched.

"*Ndonga*!" she suddenly called in a panic. "Quick, fetch Juma at once!"

The boy, scared at seeing his father stretched out in bed at that hour, raced out and ran through the maize field towards Juma's house, hoping he had returned home from the factory.

Luckily Juma was at home, bathed and dressed in his old wool coat, preparing to leave for Kampi Nyasi after the day's work.

He hurried through the maize field after the boy, anxious for his friend.

A while later, supporting the ill man between him and Njambi, they set off towards Kampi Nyasi. There was a little clinic in the village run privately by a nurse who worked for the Nairobi City Council by day. They hoped she was already back from work, and that the place was open.

***

Back at the main house JP's wife Njeri was a maimed tigress. She had been that way the entire evening, ever since her return from her usual day's work managing the string of eating joints she operated on Tom Mboya Street in Nairobi, on top of a hardware store in Gikomba.

Apparently a deal they had been working on for the supply of construction material to a government firm that was expanding in the Community area had been grabbed from under her feet. It was a project that involved good money spread out over a couple of years, and which she had been pushing patiently, prodding JP to craftily turn the many bolts along the tedious process. And now, at the brink of the whole thing, someone else had snatched the opportunity.

And what beat her was the apparent helplessness of her husband in the face of it all.

"You can't think of anything inside that fat head of yours, is that what you are saying?" thundered Njeri, her hands planted on her full hips.

She was a stunningly beautiful woman; there was no doubt about it. Her well filled body was proportioned perfectly, not too thin, and not too fat either. Her fair cocoa skin, the gentle rise of her faintly ringed neck, and dark sparkly eyes that pinned a man down with their powerful feminity had always stunned JP. Standing in the soft bedside light in her silky nightgown that came just up to her knees, and which moulded her huge bust and wide hips in those shadowy cascading lines, further adding profile to her sensuous curves...she was...beautiful.

JP sat on a footstool at the far end of the room with his gaze lowered to the already turned out bed. He was stripped down to his jockey shorts, and there was a boyish look of uncertainty on his sweaty face, his lower lip wet from repeated nervous licking. He was conscious of their son Gaitho still up watching a late movie in the TV room further down the corridor, and who might overhear them. He wished her rage would boil over, at least for tonight, for he desperately wanted her.

"Eh? Won't you speak up?" she said, advancing, her hand outstretched. "What is it that you can ever do right, you little fool? Why is it that with everything you do someone must constantly look over your shoulder to guide you? Eh? What is it you have in that fat head of yours? Can't you fix such a simple matter as this? Eh? And yet you call yourself an important man- a *Mheshimiwa* indeed!"

JP, stung to the bone, hang his head in shame.

"Here," she persisted, engaging that higher gear in this routine argument that he knew too well, her outstretched palm sticking underneath his nose. "What do you have for me, you fat fool!" she spat, bending low so she was speaking directly into his face. Her voice had risen a note higher in her agitation, a familiar raw razor edge to every word that spelt terror.

JP licked his dry lips yet again and rose to his feet; his rounded shoulders that were normally hunched now dropping. In the shambly walk of the dumb boy in the school yard who everyone poked fun at he walked slowly to where he had left his clothes on a pile in the bedside armchair. Groping in his leather jacket he took out a thick wad of notes rolled carefully and tied down with a rubber band. Walking hesitantly, he brought the money over to his wife.

His darting eyes, that he couldn't bring to rest on her, told his utter desperation.

She snapped up the money and moved up to the light, where she proceeded to count the used bills meticulously one after the other.

He watched her in silence, his anxiety mounting slowly as she came to the end of the wad.

He knew who was behind the last minute switch in the tender award, and was well aware that there was nothing he could do. He had been threatened before, and he had been in the Party long enough to know how the hierarchy of internal power and influence worked. And his powerful foe's upper hand was all too obvious in the matter. The many incidences in the recent past where the man had gone to all lengths to ground his adversaries, hounding them not just out of public office but even going further and grinding down their personal investments were well known. One simply didn't take chances with a person like that.

"Only this?" Njeri suddenly spun around, waving the wad of notes angrily in his face. "This is all that you made for me the whole of today?" She advanced slowly in his direction, her round face warping up in anger, eyes narrowing. And it was with that cold lowered voice that chilled his blood that she addressed him. "You don't want me to shut the gates on your trucks at the auction, do you, fat man? Eh? You don't want that now, do you? You know it will only take a phone call," she jerked her hand next to her ear for effect, warm breath hissing on his face. "A *phone call*, that's what!"

JP, with the fear of death itself now in his narrowed eyes, slid down to the floor and roped his arms about her loins, his sweaty face buried in her perfumed groin, gasping imploringly. "Don't do that, my dear. Please don't. You know that I love you dearly, and that I will do anything you ask, *murata*..."

"Don't *'murata'* me, hear?" she snapped reproachfully after watching him whimper for a while. "You know you sicken me up to here when you do that!" she said in a biting tone that would be used on an imbecile, gesturing with her index finger beneath her ringed chin. "Get up! ...Out- that way!" she stabbed her finger at the connecting door beside the one that led to the bathroom.

A look of fear washed over JP's crestfallen face at the command, his shoulders sagging further. And as he rose and hurried off to the dark little room where his narrow cot was, his hopes for a sensual night in her soft arms dashed, she mouthed an expletive after him, her face twisted in the snarl of the Angel of Death.

After the door was latched shut she turned and walked to the gilt-edged oval mirror mounted on her Queen Anne clubfoot dresser. Behind the hinged mirror was a square safe door with a combination lock. She spun the dial and turned the knob, revealing a square chamber stacked with rows of bank notes. She placed the money inside, carefully arranging the row, and then closed the door.

It was as she was preparing to slip underneath the quilt spread on the big four-poster bed after a visit to the bathroom that the chime of the ringer echoed through the mazework of corridors that penetrated the expansive house. The whispery sound no longer emanated from the TV room, meaning Gaitho had long gone to bed.

Turning over, she called through the wall, "JP... eeee...? Wake up! Go and see who it is at the door! Probably one of your stupid workers!"

And then she rolled onto her side under the covers and snapped out the light.

***

The wealthy farm-owner kept muttering angrily under his breath as the car banged along the rut-marked road on the way to Kikuyu. He was driving rather fast, his squinted eyes glued to the road ahead that was lit by the long shafts of the headlamps, which stabbed the enveloping blanket of darkness. Seated beside him was his bodyguard, a tall rather quiet Kalenjin who had been allocated to him, and who stayed in one of the outhouses at the back of the house.

In the back of the Range-Rover Juma and the peasant couple sat in mute silence. Propped up between his wife and the farm overseer the ill man was a pale sight, head hung forward over his chest, face pale and an ashen colour. His equally pale tongue snaked out of his cracked lips with every chest-heaving gasp for breath, and every time that weak hoarse cough that boomed inside his hollow-sounding chest came he clasped his frail arms tighter about the shoulders of his minders, as if the last hour was truly nigh. At the end of it his wife would dab tenderly at the strings of spittle flaking his mouth with the edge of her *lesso* cloth. He had grown thinner and aged within a couple of days. Deep shadows had appeared on his unshaven cheeks, his eyes retreating into their sockets.

84

In the frightful silence hardly anyone spoke, save for JP's angry muttering as he wrestled with the car, banging it torturously along the rough road.

At long last the twin beams of the headlights swung off the road and into the hospital entrance.

They carried Yakobo out of the car and placed him in a wheelchair, wheeling him down the brightly-lit hall.

As the cheerful orderly took him into the examination room, the dumbstruck Njambi hurried along, watching his face frightfully. JP and the bodyguard remained in the reception area, JP pacing up and down impatiently, declining the Styrofoam cup of lukewarm coffee the sisters offered.

They were long in there, and JP was starting to get fidgety, glancing at his watch now and then. It was well past midnight. And yet, when he thought about the house and the narrow bed in the dark little chamber that awaited him he found that it was not worthy anticipating at all. And so he spilt out his frustrations on the bodyguard.

"What is keeping those people in there?" he shouted, banging his hand palm-down on the reception desk. "They think we are here to wait for them all night?"

"I don't know, *Mzee*. Perhaps they decided to have him admitted..." said the tall Kalenjin guard, eager to put his new boss at ease.

"Well, can't you go in there and find out!" snapped back JP, doffing his hat and scratching at his shiny scalp. "You think I for a while enjoy being feasted on by mosquitoes out here?"

"In a moment, *Afande!*"

The guard disappeared into the corridor.

Across the waiting hall cartoon characters darted

mutely across a TV set mounted on the wall to keep the visitors occupied, their animated movements jerky and out of this world. A thin old woman in a starched hospital frock sat huddled on one of the benches, facing the TV. She wasn't watching the programme but was nodding off, as her head that kept dropping and jerking back upright indicated. Perhaps she was unable to go to sleep in her own bed.

Two hospital guards sat in the shadows at the far end, nursing Styrofoam cups, at a loss for stories to pass the hours.

JP took out a slim pack of imported cigarettes and wandered outside into the cool night, striking a match.

He smoked with long deep draughts that betrayed his nervousness, looking out into the cool night.

When the cigarette was half finished he dropped it on the cement and crushed it with the heel of his boot. The sister seated behind the little cubicle overlooking the reception was watching him in silence, knowing well there was little she could say to the MP.

As he stomped back into the hall the foursome appeared in the brightly-lit corridor, accompanied by the hospital matron.

"Well, what took you people so long?" demanded JP in his high authoritative voice, glancing at his gold wristwatch.

Yakobo, holding onto Juma for support, was led to one of the benches in the hall and sat down.

"I have examined this patient, and I must say he is not in a good state. He is very ill, and needs close attention," said the sister, addressing JP. She was clutching a clipboard to her bust, on which she had made some notes.

"*Ehe*? I am listening," said JP, meeting the white sister's gaze.

"In our thinking he shouldn't be let out of the hospital at all. We need to put him under constant surveillance to see how the drugs we have administered respond. We would prefer if he was admitted in the ward."

"I suppose he would foot the bill himself," interjected JP coolly, guessing where the story was leading.

"I have spoken to the wife," continued the sister, the hard look on her face hardly altering. "They both seem helpless. Apparently they don't have any money. Indeed the man himself seems unwilling. I am therefore appealing to you as the employer to give your consent so that we can admit him." There was that look of controlled patience on the sister's face that suggested she was not new to handling recalcitrant charges.

For a while JP and the tall sister eyed each other, as if squaring for a fight.

"Listen, sister," said JP, drawing up to his full height. "Already I am sacrificing my sleep being here at this hour. It was only out of concern that I accepted to leave my warm bed and drive this man here- like any Good Samaritan would. However, if it is only a matter of admitting him into the ward, then why don't you go ahead? I don't think we'll stay up all night discussing such a simple matter as that."

"Is that alright with you, Njambi?" the matron turned to the sick man's wife.

But it was Yakobo who stirred first, making an effort to sit up straight on the bench. Gazing fixedly at his confused wife he slowly shook his head in an emphatic no. "*Ah-ah!*" he whispered through cracked lips, his yellowed eyes shifting to the white matron. "I want to go home." His voice was an emphatic croak, and at the end of the sentence his protruding Adam's apple jerked in his throat as he swallowed the dry clog that wouldn't be cleared.

"You see?" said JP, a shade triumphantly, fat arms held out in the manner of a trick artist who has just pulled something out of the hat. "The man himself doesn't want to go to the ward, so, what do we do?" There was a bemused look on his moist round face.

"I am putting this to you, Mr. King'ong'o," said the sister, her face hardening even more. "This man is *ill*, and he probably doesn't know what he is saying. You *must* give your consent for him to be admitted in the ward; *now!*"

There was a moment of uncomfortable silence in which JP looked in turn from one to the other of his workers. Then he turned sharply and signaled the guard with a finger. "Let's go home. I think I am wasting my time here listening to this *muthungu* sister. I don't think we understand each other. As for you, Madam, these people are all yours. You can do with them as you please...just don't involve me, understood?"

With that he turned and stormed out of the hospital, followed by his bodyguard.

They had hardly reached the car in the parking lot when the rest followed, the patient hobbling weakly between his wife and the farm overseer.

Silently they climbed into the car.

And as the Range Rover pulled out of the parking area with a screech of tires the white matron and a nurse who had attended to the ill farmhand watched in shocked silence from the hospital entrance, silhouetted against the bright lighting in the hall.

"*Jinga sana!*" spat JP as he aimed the Range Rover through the narrow entranceway and slammed his foot on the gas.

Chapter Nine

YAKOBO coughed and turned over onto his side, causing the creaky bed to squeak in protest. He was covered with sweat from head to toe, and the beddings were soaked, emitting a sharp pungent smell. But still the sweat poured from his skin.

The fever had gone down a bit after the medication he had been given at the hospital. But still, occasionally, it would resurface with a vengeance. In that brief moment he would clasp his thin frame as the narrow bed went *trrrr...!*, the shivering accentuated by the startled termites drumming their brown heads angrily on the infested bed frame.

And then the moment would pass and the room would be still again.

Yakobo's medication was placed on the stool by the bed; a few aspirin and paracetamol tablets wrapped up in old newspaper. Beside the parcel was a plastic tub half full of water. There was a bowl of gruel on the table that he had given up trying to force down his throat the moment Njambi had left with the children for work.

It had long cooled, a hard scab forming on the surface, split by a giant jagged crack down the middle. Air bubbles trapped under the scab resembled the skin of a field toad. Over the long crack fruit flies buzzed, occasionally settling and crawling inside, before taking to the air again.

He had no appetite for anything.

Yet again Yakobo turned over and this time he attempted to rise to his elbow. His lips and throat

were parched; he urgently needed a drink of the
water in the tub. But then, as he tried to reach for
the tub his strength failed him, and he fell back on
the hard stuffed mattress with a groan, the sweat that
had sprang out of his skin at the effort soaking into
the straw in the lumpy stuffed mattress. He wished
Njambi and the children were here to attend to him.
His strength seemed to have deserted him all at once,
leaving him utterly helpless.

A fresh bout of spasms came all of a sudden and
his whole body shook violently, his torso thrust off the
bed, clenched teeth chattering. Giant beads of sweat
popped up on his forehead and the thin patched
blanket slid to the floor.

Then it passed and he stayed on his back, panting
softly as he regained his breath, arms stiff as ramrods
by his side. His eyes were giant yellow balls that
protruded from his skull, turning slowly above the
jutting cheekbones, surveying the room.

He took in the details of the room he had built
from scrap with the help of his friend Juma in that
rainy year he had come to live on the farm. He took in
the rotting cardboard walls that were plastered with
old newspapers, the newsprint slowly turning yellow
and brittle as the paper gave in to the ravaging smoke
and heat of the years. He took in the neat round holes
punctured in the newsprint by the giant roaches living
in the gaps in the rotting boards, and which were
looking to get at the scabbed *chapati* flour paste that
had been used to glue the newspapers to the walls. He
took in the scrap metal roof that still spread faithfully
over their heads, protecting them from the weather in
the succeeding seasons, now sagging in the middle as
the rot got to the soot-covered rafters.

He watched a giant fly zap in and out of a column of

light running down from a hole in the roof to a spot on the beaten floor. It seemed to enjoy its game because it disappeared for a while, and then reappeared to start all over again.

Yakobo wished he had *just* an ounce of that strength the fly was wasting on its purposeless game; just enough to get up and reach for the tub of water.

As midday approached the fever got worse. His body temperature was alarmingly high, and his lips were dry and scaly, jaws locked together. The headache hammered on, threatening to split his head in two. And as he gasped in lungfuls of air the wind rasped painfully at the back of his constricted throat. He was very weak, but he knew that he must summon up strength and reach for the water.

In a moment of fright he forced his gummy lips open and gave a cry for help. A croaky whisper escaped his lips, but went no further than the cardboard walls. A scary silence surrounded him.

The only respondent to his cry for help was a little gecko that lived behind the old newspapers on the wall above the stove, which now came out of hiding and stayed there, staring at him with glassy amphibian eyes, scimitar tongue darting in and out of its mouth.

With an immense force of will Yakobo heaved and rose to his elbow, the room swirling round and round before his eyes. He was panting harshly, his jaw hanging slack with the terrible thirst, yellowed tongue hanging out.

In the near madness induced by his condition a hazy illusion played in his mind's eye, the grains of the out-of-focus picture pushing against the back of his pulsing eyelids. It was the picture of his children running in the meadow down by the river, the rolling grass green with the first fall of rain, pink and white poppies springing out of the dirt where their seeds had lain in wait through the dry months.

And as they came closer the laughing faces slowly transformed into giant flies butting against a spotted glass barrier, the rasp of their wings and limbs filling his head, sounding like the crunch of sun-dried locust carapaces underfoot. The multi-coloured poppies turned into jagged-edged bleached bones and fat green worms wriggling out of the rotting belly of the earth, their tiny button faces mocking the fly, waiting for it to tire out and drop.

Yakobo squeezed his eyes shut and opened them again, renewing his effort to get at the water, determined not to succumb to the hysteria that clawed at his frazzled nerves.

The bedside stool swam in and out of his vision like a mirage on the brink of harsh wasteland, the newspaper bundle that contained the aspirin close, and yet far, unreachable. It was all like a dim light at the end of a winding tunnel that he must crawl through. He was weak, almost to the point of death. But refusing stubbornly to succumb, he yet again summoned up his waning strength and reached for the water, tipping over to the edge of the bed.

As his hands clawed towards the dancing white tub he felt an enormous wave of dizziness wash over him.

He rolled over and fell to the hardpan floor.

***

They found him later in the evening, arm folded trapped underneath him, head resting on one side, slimy yellow saliva drooling from his half-open mouth. There was a pained expression of stubborn resoluteness on his face, which had turned a pale ashen colour in death.

Chapter Ten

JUMA sat outside his friend's hut and sipped from the calabash of millet porridge, gazing out to the other end of the trampled yard where the fresh grave was. At the other end the children played, Ndonga laughing gleefully from up the gnarled guava tree while Mukami pleaded at the foot of the tree, unable to climb up to her brother's level. Their heads were clean-shaven, angry puss-filled sores popping all over their scalps where the razor had grazed the skin, attracting flies.

Beyond the little yard the maize was fully-grown, the cobs fat, starting to draw the birds, which perched on the choicest and proceeded to tear it open even before the farmer could taste the harvest of his labour. Above them the dried crowns stood stiffly in the breeze, their unyielding curled fingers like dead talons, barren of pollen.

Juma looked beyond the maize at the thick grey clouds that were slowly gathering in the purple evening sky, stretching languidly across the horizon. They would have to harvest the field sooner than they had expected, otherwise if the late season rains were to set in, then the crop would be ruined.

It was strange how the seasons came these days. Only the cabbage seemed to get the timing right.

Mama Ndonga emerged from the hut with her bowl of porridge and sat down on the beat verge of earth, leaning against the weatherworn wall of the house.

"Ndonga! Mukami!" she called at the noisy children.

"*Eee...*Mama!" chorused the two, pausing in their play.

"I say, come and eat up your porridge, you stubborn children! Now you are playing with food, you don't even know if tomorrow you will have to make do with just water in your rumbly bellies!"

The two had abandoned their porridge at Juma's feet as they ran off to play.

Juma watched them in silence, conscious of the strain in the widow's voice even as she tried to appear cheerful. Things must be getting tougher in the house now that Yakobo was no longer here. He had watched her struggle to keep up the conversation with the other village women earlier in the day as they had moved among the coffee bushes. He was not for once deceived by her forced humour. He wondered what he could do to help. He hoped the harvesting of the maize would come sooner so that he could donate part of the allowance JP's wife usually extended to him to her. He would easily make do with a quarter a bag himself.

The tiny yard around the house was yet to recover, the grass trampled underfoot in the weeklong ceremony that had preceded the burial, in which the mourners had descended on the home, drumming and dancing. Juma was certain that Njambi had exhausted all the food in the house hosting them.

"They are getting harder of hearing, these children," said Juma, breaking the silence.

"I tell you- and it is all Yakobo's making. I used to tell him to cane this Ndonga to straighten him a little, but always he would side with the boy, saying he was not old enough for the cane. The man had a soft spot for the boy, is true- he really loved him. But then that was just where the problem lay. Now he is ever getting into mischief. He worries me, indeed."

"I'm sure he'll straighten up as he grows, Njambi. Really that is the way of boys. You needn't worry too much about him."

"Aha! And so you too are in league with your friend! I say, this boy needs to have a good spanking on the bottom once in a while. *That* is what is going to straighten him. And I intend to do just that. Those long legs deceive him, making him feel he is too big for me. Well, he has got it all wrong!"

Not knowing what to say Juma sipped his porridge slowly, swirling the calabash slowly round and round.

Njambi stared for a while across the yard, her porridge steaming away in her hands, thoughts lost in the fading grey horizon. Then she snapped out of it and took a long drag of her porridge, swallowing slowly. "Juma, it is good you came by to see us this evening," she said, licking the grain residue on her lip. "I was really hoping to talk to you. There's something I wanted to tell you."

"*Ehe*? I am listening," said Juma, turning around on the low folding chair.

Njambi took her time, taking another long drag from the bowl and swallowing, licking the smear on her lips. "I have been thinking a lot this week, especially following the departure of the mourners. I think I am going to leave the farm."

"What-?" Juma was clearly caught by surprise at the pronouncement.

"Yes," said Njambi softly, nodding as if to herself, her lips sucked in decisively. "I am going to leave the farm soon. I have been thinking about my sister's proposal at the funeral. It has been giving me many restless nights. I think she was right. Perhaps I need to try my luck elsewhere."

"But why?" said Juma, struggling to digest the

information. "I mean, there's still work enough on this farm, and in any case you know we are here to help you, I mean, I don't understand-"

"You cannot understand," said Njambi softly, gazing into the distance. "At least not unless you are living in this house."

"Well, enlighten me. I must say I am surprised to hear it."

In the ensuing silence as she organized her thoughts the widow kept her gaze trained on the darkening sky, surveying the long pink streak lining the bottom of the heavy clouds. "Juma, it is only a few days since your friend's departure, and already his absence is being felt. It is getting difficult feeding the children, and really I don't see how I am going to manage on what we earn on the farm. Already I have too many debts I need to settle with people around here...*Ah-ah!*," she said with a slow shake of the head. "I just don't see how I am going to make it."

"Njambi_" But the words Juma had meant to say dried on his lips. He remained staring across at the children playing, oblivious of their mother's predicament.

"Juma, I don't think there's need to deceive myself. My eyes are open and my mind is very clear. If I stay here I will soon become a burden to good people like you. I must prepare to leave." She swallowed, lifting her gaze from the horizon for a while to confirm the words with her listener. But when she saw that he was shy of meeting her eyes, she lifted them back to the comfort of the darkening distance.

"My sister says the flower farm where she works pays better. I will give it a try. Already Yakobo and I were running debts here, and so, what about now that I am on my own, and with the children getting older? No, I must leave and search for a future for them elsewhere. Maybe out there Ndonga will even be able to get a little education and make something of his life, who knows? Maybe the chance is waiting out there for one of these children. We can't all stay trapped in this cycle for generations to come, passing the same to our children. No, I think I will take this step now, while I still can."

Joshua watched his friend's widow for a while, noting the set of her face. She had made up her mind. Somehow, he knew she wasn't going to be dissuaded.

He finished his porridge in silence and rose, walking off towards the valley, hardly saying a word to her.

***

It was cold and drizzly for a Sunday morning. The mid-year sunny spell had passed, and now the grey clouds were slowly gathering, locking out the sun that had ripened the coffee beans and sweetened the tomatoes and *ngwaci* on the tiny farms down by the valley.

Njambi sat on the bare wooden bed contemplating. The stuffed old mattress was rolled up and tied with sisal string into a handy bundle, resting on the floor beside the carton boxes that contained all their possessions. The lone chair was folded and stacked on one of the cartons. The stool had been turned upside down, and in the narrow space between the legs stuffed the well-folded clothes and the patched blanket, a sisal string tied in a loose x over the bulging sides in a manner that would be easy to carry with one hand.

The children could be heard playing in the yard outside, already bathed and dressed in their best clothes. Now all that remained was for Juma to arrive, and then they would be going on their way.

They needed to start early because, while Kiambu was only an hour's walk from the farm, it would be much further with loads on their heads.

They were going to Njambi's sister's place, a little wooden shack on the outskirts of the town that she had agreed to share with them until they found work on the flower farm and a new place of their own.

As Njambi waited, she reflected on her situation. She was virtually penniless, having cleaned out the account she had been running with her husband at the local Post Office to carter for the funeral expenses. The only money she had was what they had collected the day before for their daily wage, and which was tied up in a corner of her *lesso*. She had no grain either, which they would need to sustain them until their next pay at the end of the week.

And as usual, when she thought about this, memories of Yakobo came flooding back. How so easy it would have been had he been around. Even though they wouldn't have much money, at least they wouldn't lack for other every-day commodities like milk and flour. It was easy for one to give up on life at such moments...

In the steady drizzle pattering on the old roof she reached for the edge of her *lesso* and squeezed her watering eyes, blowing her nose.

It was a relief when Juma's whistle sounded outside.

The children ran up to greet him and, holding onto his hands, ushered him into the house.

"Sorry I am late, Mama Ndonga. The service took forever to come to an end," said Juma, shaking water from his raincoat. "And on top of that, as usual the Gachie bus just wouldn't come on time!"

"It is alright, Juma. It's still early," she said with

a smile, which nevertheless still wouldn't clothe the apprehension she felt inside. She started readying everything so that they could leave.

"You are sure you don't want to give it another try, Mama Ndonga?" said Juma, sizing up the packed bundles. "Things might not work out to your expectations where you are going. At least here we can find ways of getting by."

The cold look she gave him told him it was the wrong thing to say at the time.

"I am sorry, Njambi. I didn't mean to discourage you. All the same, I really don't like to see you go, that is for sure. I really had gotten used to you people; you were like family."

Coughing in the uncomfortable silence that had fallen he went over to the bundles and took up the metal trunk and lifted it onto his shoulder. In the other hand he took up the stool and stooped low to pass out of the house. Njambi took up the mattress and carton box. Ndonga carried the stove, and Mukami a little bundle of clothes tied up in an old headscarf.

The drizzle kept up as the little party made their way through the maize field, ducking underneath tall maize stalks that leaned into the way. For some reason, now that they were on their way a heavy silence had descended. Even Ndonga, who usually liked to make fun of Juma whenever he came visiting, seemed to know that they were onto something clandestine, and clammed up. Indeed he had intended to ask his mother just where it was they were going with all their stuff packed up, and if at all they would be coming back to visit.

But then, somehow, he knew it was not a time for asking questions. And so he followed silently at the end of the trail, hoping that wherever it was they were going would be more fun, and that there would be many interesting lads to play with compared to the rather drab lot at the farm.

At the fringe of the maize field, however, just before they got into the line of trees that lined the farm fence all the way to the main gate Njambi stopped to glance back one last time at the place she had called home all these years. She looked towards the zinc-and-timber shack, leaning at an angle against the landscape, standing rather forlornly at the end of the field. Only the gnarled stunted guava tree besides was there to keep it company.

Her eyes followed the narrow winding path that ran from it through the maize field up to the cattle *boma*, and then on to the main house, which, from where they stood, was partly hidden behind a grove of giant banana trees. This path that had been beaten by her husband, springing out of bed in the middle of the night and racing up to the cattle *boma* to deliver a calf; or just dashing off to some emergency at the main house.

Juma's house stood deeper in the maize field where the land sloped towards the river. The narrow path that ran from it to the bridge could not be seen from where they stood because the maize on that side was tall and knit. Further beyond the muddy river snaking its way through the valley Kampi Nyasi village was a long flat swathe of burnt sawgrass on the periphery. Tiny columns of smoke curled heavenward from the long thatched blocks that housed not just Chapa Kazi Farm's workforce, but the myriad dependants; petty traders, village shylocks, handymen and alley whores; all of whom drew their livelihood from the coffee money.

Ndonga had stopped too and was following his mother's gaze. He knew what she was thinking...She was thinking about his father. She had been doing that a lot lately.

...Well, he missed him too. It had been fun with Dad around, there was no doubt. He remembered him walking with them through the maize fields on Sunday afternoons during the sunny months towards Christmas. Usually Mukami would be sitting astraddle his shoulders, Ndonga running alongside, chewing a piece of sugarcane he had brought them from their aunt's place in Banana. Sometimes they would be piping off shrilly from the whistles he had cut for them from dry river reeds, and which would send the birds in the field scattering in a scare.

Right then, with the late afternoon sun shining through the tall cypresses on the fringe of the field in countless parallel shafts, the maize would be dark and green, just preparing to bring out their crowns; which peeked through the rolled tender leaves at the top of the stalk like tufts of dust-coated hair inside an old man's nostril. The succulent stems would be fat like riverside sugarcane, the broad leaves swaying gently in the breeze. On the pleasant afternoon breeze would be the perfume of the coffee flowers, for the coffee trees at the fringe of the maize field would be in full bloom, the scent drawing many insects, which buzzed around the bushes like bees.

Ndonga looked towards the spot by the house where his father's grave was slowly being overgrown by grass. He could see it clearly from where they were standing through a parting in the long maize stalks. It was a spot he liked to avoid the way one would a small black snake coiled on a bush.

At that moment his mother nudged him, snapping him back into the present, and they walked on into the trees after the other two.

***

Back at the farmhouse JP was not in the best of moods for a Sunday morning. He had just had a quarrel with his wife Njeri over the milk money before she had left for church. On top of that the newspaper boy had not delivered the paper, meaning he could not update himself on the proceedings at the funds drive his party had conducted in a neighbouring constituency towards construction of cattle dips, which he had skipped because of other business. And yet he was eager to know what his political adversary had achieved with the Party heads.

Seeing as the drizzle outside hardly permitted a stroll through the garden there seemed little to do but sit and wait for the weather to lift. It was a pity his son, Gaitho, had already left for his studies in the US. They might have enjoyed a game of draughts by the fire.

There was little doubt that he would be hitting the bottle early today.

He went to the mini bar in the TV room on the upper landing and poured himself a keg of Tusker. Carrying the frothing mug he strolled out through the sliding doors onto the rooftop terrace that jutted over the western wing of the house, slipping into one of the contour Adirondack chairs underneath the parasol. He took a long drag of the beer and rested the mug on the broad rain-spattered armrest, belching.

It was as he leaned back into the seat that he saw the movement at the fringe of the maize field, which from that height rolled out into the mist-shrouded distance. Looking closely, he discerned the foursome making their way into the trees.

Of course it was a Sunday, the day the farmhands took off work to go to church, or to visit their relations. But then what arrested his attention were the bundles the foursome were carrying, and the route they had taken.

It must be Yakobo's widow and the children, thought JP as he climbed down to the hall, where the green phone that was linked to another in the guardroom was. A strange stirring had started deep inside him even as he dialed.

"Sempei!" he barked into the phone, brushing beer froth from his lip.

"*Epa!*" said the Maasai guard at the other end, no doubt startled out of a doze by the charcoal brazier in the hut.

"You are not sleeping on the job now, are you, you *kipofu* guard?"

"No, *Mdosi*. We are very alert...*Kabisa!*"

"Alert indeed! And yet you don't know what is going on just a few yards from your hut!"

There was a dry silence at the other end, the startled guard swallowing nervously.

"*Ehe!* Go on, lie to me, Sempei. People are moving in and out of the farm just under your nose- just what am I paying you people for, tell me!"

In the uncomfortable silence JP downed a swallow of beer and slapped the mug angrily back on the desk, spilling some of the contents. "Go out to the trees towards the cattle *boma* at once and see who those four are. They are leaving the farm by that lower *panya* entrance I ordered you people to close...*haraka!* Stop them until I get there, hear?" JP's whining voice had upped a tempo in agitation.

"*Epa!* Right away, *Mdosi!*"

JP slammed the phone down and heaved himself up the stairs to get his shoes and a coat. Shortly he reappeared, dangling the car keys, his Stetson slouched at an angle over his shiny bald head. He walked through the connecting door and as he climbed into the Range Rover parked beside the navy Mercedes in the double-door garage he thumbed the tiny black button on the wall that operated the electric garage door. The door wound upwards with a whine, the corrugated steel sheet coiling up inside its housing with a dry crunch. Shifting gears he sent the Range Rover roaring out into the slanting drizzle.

***

The narrow path wound through the wattle trees and ended at a low wooden gate, which was nailed shut with crossbeams. For a long while casual hands taken on to help pick the coffee had used the entrance. JP had ordered it closed when he attempted to introduce the clock on the farm, where every worker had to clock in and out of work. For some reason the system hadn't worked. Part of the reason being once the workers had clocked in, they hardly made an effort to produce, knowing all they needed for the day to be entered was clock out at the end of it. Meanwhile they were free to play hide and seek with Juma.

That was before the idea of paying them according to the level of produce they brought in at the end of the day occurred to him. Now all the workers had to enter through the main gate and assemble at the tool shed to be allocated their work for the day.

Next to the boarded up gate, like sheep that refused to give up a habit, the farmhands had soon after cut another narrow entrance through the barbed wire fence. They sneaked in through this entrance whenever they reported late. It opened out onto the road on the other side.

The by then thoroughly soaked four crept through the *panya* opening onto the muddy road.

Shortly before JP's Range Rover swept round the bend and screeched to a stop in front of them.

"Good morning! Rather late for the Sunday service the four of you, aren't you?" said the smiling farm-owner, leaning out of the open window. His fat jowled face was resting on a beefy forearm, shifty little eyes scrutinizing the startled farmhands with a mixture of suspicion and amusement. "Or were you headed somewhere else?" he said, eyebrows rising slightly as his gaze roved slowly over the loads they were carrying. "Huh? Seems to me like that might just be the case... Eh? Juma, is it?" he said at length, switching off the motor and climbing out of the car.

And as JP got out of the car a rustle was heard in the trees behind them. In the shifting bushes the Maasai guards stood spread out in a semi-circle, leaning on their long white sticks, watching silently.

"Juma!" called JP, his calf-leather shoes squelching in the mud as he approached.

"*Eee*, Boss!" said Juma, lowering his load to the wet ground and snapping to attention.

JP approached, his bloodshot eyes roving over the startled foursome. He stopped in front of the storekeeper, his appraising gaze resting on the woman and children.

The drizzle pattered on his coat and slid down in tiny rivulets, the tan leather resisting a soak. His patent leather shoes, clearly not made for the conditions, were rimmed with red mud, the shiny leather beaded with tiny droplets of water.

"Where are you going?" he said at length, his gaze finally shifting to the dumbstruck storekeeper. "*You* are not taking off with the widow, are you? At least not this early, before the grave is overgrown with grass?"

His thin smile widened an inch at his own bland humour.

"Er, Boss.... Sh-she asked me to help her carry her belongings to her cousin's place..."

"Is she leaving already? *Uh*? Tired of working on the farm?" There was a look of mild surprise on JP's face as his gaze slowly shifted to the woman.

"That's right. I thought I could try my hand at something else," supplied Njambi, seeing that Juma was at a loss.

"You'd like to try your hand at something else," said JP slowly, nodding as if divulging the information syllable by syllable.

"That's right, *Mzee*," affirmed Njambi in the uncomfortable silence. "I really don't think I will be able to raise the children single-handedly working on the farm."

"I see." JP took a step back and pushed his left hand into his pocket, the other hanging by his side, dangling the car keys more the way a child would a rattle. Up above in the knit canopy the drizzle pattered, the icy droplets falling through the wet leaves in a staggered staccato. "You are tired of the place, eh? Mama Ndonga?"

"Not quite, *Mzee*..."

"Or is it you have made enough money out of this farm you now want to get out to start your own *biashara*?"

"Ahmmm... Not quite..."

"What is it then, waYakobo? Did anyone treat you badly here?" In the ensuing silence in which the widow groped for words the wealthy farm owner circled slowly in the mud, surveying them and the luggage they carried. It was getting most uncomfortable to be scrutinized in that way.

"Aha!" he exclaimed at length, wiping his moist round face and nodding in the manner of someone who has stumbled upon a discovery after lengthy thought. "It is quite understandable, all the same," he nodded, swallowing a plug of phlegm that had gathered at the back of his throat. "Indeed people need a change once in a while. It is only *kawaida.*"

Yet again he surveyed each one of them carefully, the car keys clanging on the swaying ring hooked on his index finger, nodding his head in comprehension.

"But then, one would expect, lady, that you would at least let your employer know you were leaving?" he spun around suddenly, an icy steeliness in his eyes, that now came to rest squarely on Njambi. "Why the silent *sneaking* out, Mama Ndonga, eh? Why? ...Why this unusual route?"

"Er...Ah..." her throat gone dry all of a sudden, Njambi fidgeted on her feet, trying to find the words. Beside her the clearly uncomfortable Juma was wringing his hands, his gaze trained on the muddy ground.

"...You didn't want to bother the *tajiri* this early in the morning, I suppose was the reason. Quite understandable too," quipped JP with an understanding nod.

And then he raised his head, and this time a foxy look had crept into his shifty little eyes. "Or perhaps you deliberately *didn't* have to bother the *tajiri*...is it, Mama Ndonga? Eh? That you needn't do that because you were running away from something...?"

This time Njambi started fidgeting, the confidence she had exuded earlier waning. Just what did he mean 'deliberately'? She looked at the children, still clutching their loads, looking uncertainly at their employer and back at their mother, sensing the latter's mounting fear.

"Eh? You had something to hide, Mama Ndonga?" repeated JP, drawing closer.

"Err...I don't understand, Sir," said Njambi, licking her lips nervously.

"Aha! *You* don't understand. Well, so I'll remind you." JP's gaze shifted casually from the farmhands to the posse of silent Maasai guards in the trees, as if to reassure himself that they were still there. "Indeed I will, Mama Ndonga." He gave a low cough to clear his throat and moved an inch closer, his fat index finger wagging in the misty air.

"Of course you remember your husband's illness; given it was only the other day, Mama Ndonga. It is very sad that Yakobo had to pass on. I must say he was one of my most faithful employees all the years he worked on this farm. Death is indeed a grim reaper, and it pains sometimes why he should pick on only the fine people and leave the wicked to torment the world." A look of commiseration passed over the farm-owner's face, but then it was only cursory. Shortly the hard look returned.

"You will recall too, Mama Ndonga, that you came to me for help to take Yakobo to hospital?" continued JP, a steely edge creeping into his voice.

"That I do," nodded Njambi, her frozen toes digging stiffly inside her worn canvas shoes that were soaked and soggy in the drizzle.

"Aha!" JP nodded, more the way a prizefighter backtracking for acceleration space as he prepares to charge a foe he has painstakingly coaxed into a corner would do. "Yet again it is with a lot of sadness that this farm had to lose the services of a good man. But then, even as we buried him on the farm, there was a little issue that we hadn't discussed, my lady...and with reason too. For it would have been most improper at the time, saddled with the funeral as you were."

Now the cold steeliness was all too obvious in JP's probing little eyes, his tone no longer conciliatory. As for the farmhands, like a fly that is dazzled by the body-jerking tail-flicking display of the gecko on the wall that is a precursor to certain death, they stood rooted to the spot, waiting with bated breath.

"This little matter, Mama Ndonga, is the hospital bill your husband accumulated on his subsequent visits to the hospital in Kikuyu, and which in my responsibility as employer, I shouldered for him. However," finally JP locked stares with the woman, allowing his index finger to rise a fraction, "and perhaps seeing Yakobo obviously didn't inform you, it was not for free. The arrangement with your husband, Mama Ndonga, was that he was to repay it later from his wages."

The pronouncement settled with a sinking finality, more the way a struggling bull might lower slowly to the ground at the abattoir after the last breath-gushing throe.

"You mean...," the widow searched for the words, her face gone ashen with shock at the unexpected turn.

"Yes, that was the arrangement, waYakobo," said the farm owner, cutting off her argument with a wave of the hand. "Now, Mama Ndonga, I would appreciate it if we could discuss this little matter at my house before you leave." At the snap of a finger, the crisp business tone was back in the farm-owner's voice, laying it down for the other partner's bargain.

And with that JP turned and walked off to the parked Range Rover, his expensive shoes squelching in the red mud.

Just as he reached for the door handle, he turned around and said lightly, "And I hope you don't mind the guards helping you with the luggage, seeing it is quite heavy. You will certainly do with a helping hand in this weather."

And as JP shook the rainwater off his coat and climbed into the car, the Maasai guards emerged from the trees and approached the stunned foursome, reaching for the bound up bundles. Unlike the talkative lot that they usually were every time Njambi and the children passed them at the gate, this time the guards were hardly smiling, a cloak of menace settling over their gaunt shoulders all of a sudden, faces hard and dour.

There was nothing left to do as the Range Rover ploughed a u-turn in the rut-marked road and roared off with a spray of mud. Njambi took the children by the hands and they followed the lanky guards into the trees back the way they had come.

***

Njambi stood on the stoep in front of the solid mahogany carved entrance to the farmhouse with the slanting drizzle lashing at her feet, just barely sheltered by the half-moon limestone portico over which trailing plants scrambled. She was changed into a warm cardigan, but still she trembled with the chill. JP stood in the open doorway, his huge arms crossed over his wide chest like Goliath sizing up the little man with a slingshot.

"You will give me my dues now, Mama Ndonga, and I will have absolutely no reason to keep you from going on your journey," he said judiciously, raking a fat index finger leisurely up a snotty nostril. "Even the good book says we pay back what we owe other people, you know that."

"You are right," said Njambi, nodding thoughtfully. "And you did the right thing to shoulder Yakobo's debt." Her face quivered for a while as she struggled to compose herself. "There was just no way we could have paid the hospital on our own. And, by *Ngai*, I wouldn't want to carry a debt on my head; no, I just wouldn't think of it." She nodded slowly, her brow lining with thought. "But then, I don't have that kind of money, *Mzee*," she said at length, astounded. "I can't even imagine raising it on my own!"

There was a moment of silence in which the farm owner might have been assessing the revelation, his moist face blank, save for the index finger that remained busy probing up his nostril. "Well, in that case, what do we do? I mean, it has got to be paid, Mama Ndonga." JP regarded with interest a dried green object his finger had finally managed to dislodge, before dismissively wiping it on the seat of his pants.

"You have got to give me time then to find the money," said the woman, her brow deeply lined, eyes squinted in thought.

"Well, that is fine with me, Mama Ndonga. You can take as much time as you wish, I won't rush you. You know, like I said, Yakobo was one of my fine workers; and I wouldn't want to mistreat his widow in any way where I can help it. Indeed, I am even willing to assist, if there is a way to lighten the burden," he added philanthropically, looking into the eyes of the widow. "Anything you can think of to speed up the repayment you know you have my ear, Mama Ndonga. I really would like to see you free to proceed on with your future plans; and indeed I wish you and the children well."

Njambi ground the man's words slowly through the millstones of her mind, wondering why they sounded comforting, and yet perditious all at once. In a confused daze, she gathered the folds of her old cardigan and, nodding turned and ducked into the drizzle back to the little shack in the maize plantation. It was an abrupt face-saving departure that was prompted by the need to hide her misting eyes from the farm owner.

JP stood watching her as she hurried down the garden path, his shiny eyes thoughtful. She had grown frailer since the death of her husband was true. But in the dark recesses of his plotting mind, she had grown no less attractive. Certainly no less homely.

Indeed for a fleeting while there it occurred to him how welcome it would be at that moment to have someone lift her burden for her and make things easier.

This thought slowly lifted the corner of his mouth.

Of course he was well aware of her stubborn pride that kept her short of bowing at any one's feet. Still, somehow in the remote vestiges of his mind, he knew he would be seeing her again.

Chapter Eleven

NJAMBI swallowed and stared straight ahead, boldening her heart for her employer's response.

Everything about the man's appearance told her the request would be turned down, and indeed common sense dictated so. But still she clung to the straw of hope that it would not, that there was just the slightest possibility...After all, the man had promised to help her speed up the repayment of the debt, or hadn't he?

"You say you want the boy to take over his father's place?" there was a look of clear surprise on JP's face, his eyes roving slowly over the little woman, registering her worn clothing and the tightly wound *lesso* cloth tied just above her waist. But most noticeable was her posture; pulled up to full height, shoulders held high, gaze focused. The stance of someone who will not be easily dissuaded.

"Yes, *Mzee*, I want you to take my son on," she said softly, meeting his gaze.

"Well..." He was still surprised at the way she had walked up to him as he prepared to enter the car, as if she had lain in wait in the yard a long while for him to appear. Inside the navy Mercedes his official driver waited, the engine idling.

The Kalenjin bodyguard lingered by, waiting to close the door for his boss. Inside the darkened back compartment of the limousine his beefy aide, the hard-to-miss Master, updated himself on the morning dailies.

"Well, as you see I am off to the office, woman. I don't think it is an apt time to discuss the matter," said JP, drumming his fingers softly on the freshly polished roof of the car. And yet it occurred to him that he had given his word to help a few days back.

"You can at least give it some thought, *Mzee*," persisted the woman, a slightly pleading note in her voice, even though her face remained calm and impassive.

There was a moment of silence in which JP assessed the unflinching farmhand, rearranging his thoughts.

"He can do the job perfectly well. Ndonga is a grown man now," asserted Njambi softly, conscious of the impatient bystanders, but determined to get her way nonetheless. "And," she added, "he is not going to ask for his father's wage. Ndonga will gladly take half."

She swallowed nervously, now that she had delivered her sinker.

"Well," said JP again, his dark little eyes lighting up a little, figuring. "Certainly I wouldn't give him his father's wage even if I were to take him on. You understand that he is only a boy." He scratched his freshly shaved chin slowly, his eyes narrowing. "What about milking? Who will milk the cows?"

"I", said Njambi softly.

"You?" Now the surprise was all too plain on the farm-owner's face.

"Yes, I will. First thing in the morning, and in the evening after I come back from the coffee fields."

"I see."

"I did it before, for about a week. When Yakobo's illness got worse."

"Is it?" JP nodded slowly, gazing steadily into the woman's eyes, not for a minute doubting a word of what she said. She appeared capable of close to anything.

"Besides, don't underestimate the boy. There's pretty little he still doesn't know about cows, given the time he spent in the cattle yard with his father. Maybe I won't even have to teach him anything at all!"

"I see," said JP, nodding. "And I suppose *you* know everything your husband did on the farm?" The thrifty deal-cutter edge lightly laced his words.

"Of course not, *Mzee*. I wouldn't know everything that Yakobo was capable of. But then I truly know most of the things." A dent had appeared in the woman's resolve even as she spoke.

"Well, 'knowing' is one thing, and doing it quite another," countered the wealthy man, glancing at his gold watch.

The woman waited, for a while lost for words.

"So, will you think about it, *Mzee*?" she said at length, fear clawing at her resolve at his prolonged silence.

There was that calm look in his eyes that frightened her a little. The same calm that had been there when she had gone to beg for his permission to burry her husband on the farm on that dour morning days gone by. It frightened her because it was hard to tell what he was thinking when he was that way.

"I will see," he said at last, giving a curt nod, preparing to enter the car. "Now go back to your job."

"Thank you, *Mzee*."

Njambi, awash in relief, turned and hurried off towards the tool shed, her head still held up in dignity. Behind her the door of the limousine closed and the driver gunned the motor, waiting for the bodyguard to run round to the passenger seat in the front cabin.

Chapter Twelve

In the biting chill of the dawn the boy stood in the cattle yard and looked towards the farmhouse, stifling a sleepy yawn in his hand. In the towering trees to the other side of the shed the birds chirped brightly, celebrating the dawn.

He walked into the cattle pen and moved slowly from cage to cage. He was not frightened of the huge watery bovine eyes that stared back at him from the darkness, chewing softly on the cud. He walked slowly to the far end and then back, acquainting himself.

Already he had brought out the milking cans and washed and arranged them in the scrubbed cement yard beside the feeding troughs. It was only Juma who was keeping him, for he needed to come and fix the milking machine.

It was not as if he wouldn't do it on his own. Ndonga knew pretty all there was to know about almost every piece of machinery on the farm, save for the old Massey Fergusson tractors in the yard in front of the tool shed. He had taught himself everything a boy needed to know about the machines and their workings only the way a farmyard boy could; sneaking up when a minder was looking the other way, cajoling, or simply starting them and watching, risking getting caught. It is only the old tractor-driver, a nasty fellow named Kioko, who had consistently proved difficult to charm.

And he was a distasteful old egghead too, for he wouldn't just let Ndonga sit at the wheel of his tractor, but ensured he didn't make his way into the old farm trucks as well. Kioko's word held sway when it came to anything motorized on wheels on the farm, and the drivers knew only too well not to cross his path.

As he waited for the storekeeper to come so they could commence the milking Ndonga busied himself cleaning out the feeding troughs of remnants of the previous day's feed, gathering the waste into little mounds on the floor with the stiff scrubbing broom. He went out into the yard to wheel in the heavy wheelbarrow left leaning against the shed wall. Its huge wheel and wide tray intimidated him a little, for he knew that laden with dung or nappier grass it would require even more strength and skill to hold steady on the boggy farm tracks. It was one task he had never quite mastered even as he helped his father around the farm.

As much as he was thrilled at the prospect of having to do what his dad had done, Ndonga was also not blind to the challenges. He was certain it was going to take far more than a boy's enthusiasm to fill his dad's boots.

But still he was not in the least afraid. Of that he was certain.

***

The day proved equally a drag to Mukami at the coffee estate, having to readjust to the labour. However, even as she worked among the other village children, there was a little consolation for them. The news that the little school in the village that her father and other farm workers had mooted had been reopened was exciting. And to think that her mother was in agreement with her going there after work made her even the more impatient to get there. The children were excited about learning ABCD and the barely remembered nursery-school rhymes again.

It was a relief eventually when the siren sounded from the factory building and the workers one by one assembled on the path, carrying their sack loads on their backs. Some of the naughty boys slung their sacks on the old truck that came roaring down the road and raced after it, climbing over the rickety tailgate for the ride down to the factory building.

Mukami sat at the scrubbed wooden desk a while later, her book; the torn upper half of a ruled school notebook, clutched in her sweaty hand, chewing at the stub of a pencil that her mother had given her. She was listening keenly to the young man teaching the alphabet on a piece of painted board leaning against the earth wall that served as a chalkboard. Squeezed beside her on the narrow desk were six other girls from the village, all hurriedly scrubbed and changed, still smelling of the muddy river bath, their faces glistening with anticipation.

Outside the knocking and sawing of the old carpenter from the village could be heard as he hurriedly knocked together the desks he had been contracted to make for the other class for older pupils.

And then without warning there was a loud knock at the door. The teacher, pausing in the middle of the alphabet song, went to answer it.

He spoke for a while with the person at the door, nodding repeatedly. And when he came back inside his erstwhile cheerful face was cast in shadow.

"Children, I am afraid I have some disappointing news," he said, pausing with the broken piece of wood he had been using for a ruler in his hands. "The class is dismissed. We must go back home now while the headmaster makes proper arrangements for the running of the classes," he announced sadly. He then walked over to the little table by the board and collected his book, duster and pieces of chalk.

The collective gasp that greeted the unexpected announcement was expressive of the disappointment of his eager new pupils.

But then, whatever their feelings, apparently their teacher's decision was final.

The young man, openly saddened, shrugged into his coat which had been hanging on a nail behind the door and walked out, followed by the children, who had erupted in confused chatter.

Mukami said 'bye to her friend Rose as she branched to the narrow street that led to her mother's house and walked on towards the river. Swinging her little drawstring bag from the thong around her neck, she put her thumb in her mouth and walked on solemnly on her way home.

As for the boys they hang behind a while, discussing the matter amongst themselves. One naughty boy even found a discarded piece of chalk and walked up to the chalkboard and started scribbling lines and squiggles, adjusting an invisible pair of spectacles just like the teacher. One other boy broke into the 'ABC...' song and encouraged the others to sing along as they streamed out of the class back home.

There were a few workers still about on the farm as evening approached, mostly tractor and truck drivers hauling the harvest of the day from the fields to the factory building.

As she approached the bridge, Mukami drew to the side of the road to allow the vehicle coming behind her to pass, lost in her own thoughts.

But to her surprise, the vehicle drew up beside her and stopped.

It was the farm-owner's open jeep that he usually used to tour the farm. Sitting behind the wheel was JP himself.

"Want a lift, little girl?" said the smiling farm-owner, leaning over to open the passenger door. "Hop right in! It sure is a long way to your house walking on your own."

Mukami, taken quite by surprise, hesitated. But seeing that the farm-owner really meant it, she clutched her bag to her chest and, with trembling hands, climbed up to the running board and into the cab.

The farm-owner leaned across and slammed the door. And then he stepped on the pedals, causing the car to roar in a loud vroom!

As they sped up the hump-backed bridge JP said with a bright smile, "You are not afraid of cars now, are you?" He yanked on the shiny-knobbed gear stick, causing the open jeep to spring forward.

Mukami smiled and shook her head coyly, gripping onto the car seat as they swept round a bend in the road ahead, the wind whipping over their heads.

"Aha! You won't admit it. Anyway, I can see it in your eyes, nonetheless. All kids are excited about car rides. Or don't you know that I too was once a kid – huh?"

Mukami, lost for words, gripped the doorframe and stared right ahead through the collapsible windshield, made speechless by the kindness of the rich man who would stop to let her into his car. Just wait till she got home. Ndonga was sure going to be very jealous to learn that she had been given a ride by the kind farm-owner...

"See? Now you are indeed smiling! I told you you didn't have to say it," said the farm-owner with a chuckle, humming a remembered tune that came to mind as they sped along the twisting road that wound through the wattle trees close to the homestead.

And in her rapturous excitement, the surprise closure of the school on the very day it was opened was forgotten.

***

Later that evening, after Njambi had put the children to bed and cleaned the dishes she lingered a while by the fire, roasting the nduma roots they would eat for breakfast early the following day in the smouldering embers.

As usual, when she was alone at night she found her thoughts wandering to Yakobo and memories of their earlier life. She was tired and her whole body ached from the double work she had done in the coffee fields and in the cattle *boma* helping her son. But somehow she wasn't feeling sleepy enough to retire. She knew that if she lay on the bed she would only turn from side to side, and so she stayed a while by the fire, hoping that her eyes would get heavy enough to go to sleep.

It was in the whispery stillness of the night that she heard a soft cough outside.

Stiffening, she rose, thinking it was probably Juma, coming to see if they were alright- or, precisely, if she had spared some leftover food for him by the fire. She had seen him leave in the direction of the river that evening after the milking. Probably he had gone off to Kampi Nyasi for a drink and would be hungry now.

"Who is there?" she called all the same, listening against the door. "Juma, is that you?"

But there was only silence from the other side.

"Juma?"

Mystified, and yet certain that she had heard a cough, she cast a glance at the sleeping children on the mat, before easing the rusty bolt that secured the door back, pulling it back cautiously.

"Anyone there?"

In the cool night breeze that came wafting in as her eyes adjusted, she clearly made out the figure of her visitor, darkened against the grey backdrop. He was standing with his hands buried in the pockets of his coat, the collar turned up; hat slouched low over his eyes.

"That was some nice tune you were humming in there, wa-Yakobo. I could not resist lingering a while to listen," he said softly, advancing a step and then stopping.

"We were just preparing to go to bed, *Mzee*," she said, equally in a whisper, surprised at her unexpected night-visitor.

"I see." He again coughed softly, as if measuring his words. "It is a rather still night. Ideal for a quiet moment by the fireside. The children are asleep, are they?"

"Yes. It is late as you can see."

"*Oooo*...I see." He nodded in the darkness, and yet again cleared his throat. He seemed fidgety. Njambi waited, equally nervous; suspicious. It was a long uncomfortable silence in which the night breeze rustled the maize stalks at the fringe of the yard, causing the broad leaves to sway gently. "Well, won't you invite me in?" he said at length in a low gruffy voice.

Njambi was still, a little too still because she realized her fingernails were raking into the soft wood of the door jamb, that was riddled with hundreds of tiny holes bored by the tiny insect Ndonga called the 'wood-grinder'.

"You know...," he started to say, drawing closer, perhaps encouraged by her silence.

But all of a sudden she held out her hand, palm spread. "Uh-Uhmmm! I don't think you should come in," she whispered, her tone wavery, but firm.

In the preceding static silence they glared at each other, both their eyes shining in the dark. In the gloom of the night he noticed that the surprise had lifted from her eyes, and now there was a glowing fierceness therein that could be hostility. Or fear. But certainly they were no longer friendly. The sudden change jolted him a little. "You can state your business standing right where you are, *Mzee*," she added flatly.

Her night visitor appeared to fidget on his feet a while, adjusting the slant of his wide-brimmed hat. He hawked deep in his throat, swallowing.

At length, seeing as he was not going to speak, she cleared her constricted throat and said softly, "Is *that* why you gave Mukami a lift home in your car?"

"Ahm...you are making this unnecessarily difficult wa-Yakobo, you know..." he mumbled, rather uncomfortable at the clearly unexpected turn of events.

"You still haven't answered the question...Is it?" There was a strange ring of authority in her voice that startled even herself.

And then, in the electrified silence before he could frame his answer she stepped back and pushed the door softly closed, easing the bolt back in place.

She stayed a while, leaning against the door, chest heaving as she regained her composure.

Shortly, she heard him curse softly, followed by the sound of his padded footsteps as he walked away.

Only after the night was silent again did she push herself away from the door with a sigh. She stood for a while in the middle of the hut, regaining her breath and recollecting her fragmented thoughts. Then she blew out the tin lamp and climbed noiselessly into bed, drawing the patched old blanket slowly up to her ears. The night had suddenly turned very chilly.

Chapter Thirteen

THE Alhaving stepped out of the darkness into the ring of light. In the dancing light of the tin lamp he towered high above the narrow bed, shoulders reaching up to the sagging roof, brushing the sooty tendrils hanging from the rafters. The arms that were crossed over his barrel chest were massive and hairy, thick like tree trunks. He peered over them down at her, his eyes yellow and shiny, roving left and right above the tiny snub nose and a mouth that had a feline cleft in the lower lip. The stiff whiskers framing the mouth jerked every time his broad jowls twitched. Trapped in the band of the little trilby hat perched on his head his tiny ears were pointed and plastered back against the sloping scalp.

"You look lovely when you sleep, my lady," he said in a thin whining voice that was vaguely familiar, his head cocked at an angle. "Indeed you look most pleasant." A thin pink tongue snaked out of the parting in the lower lip and licked the stiff whiskers on the hanging jowls. In the dim light the yellow canines were long and shiny, separated by a neat row of tiny equally sharp front teeth.

"Well, I'm off to my midnight walk. Mind coming along?" he said, extending a hand. "It will be worth the while, I assure you," he added in a pleasant way, a conscientious smile playing on his broad sweaty face. "Come on, you can trust my word!"

She reached to take the extended hand, the shaking of her own hand giving away the fright he instilled in her. And as her hand disappeared into the firm grasp, she realized the tightness in the grip was because the hand was indeed a paw. The bright yellow eyes stayed locked on hers, transfixing her, even as she gathered the old *rinda* that she usually slept in about her, the patched blanket slithering to the beaten floor.

As she rose she felt the old *rinda* slipping from her shoulders, as if drawn gently by an invisible hand. In its place settled a fine warm silk gown of the most elaborate cut, the fabric perfumed with jasmine and myrrh. And it fit snugly about her shoulders, as if cut specifically for her by an expert hand.

They stepped through the wall into a garden filled with trees and shrubs, all of them in full bloom. The wind whistled through the towering trees, swaying their willowy branches that reached down to touch the glassy waters of the clear spring cascading down the moss-covered rocks. In the pearly light of the moon strange multi-coloured butterflies flitted from bush to bush, filling the night with the sweet scent of the flowers. In the shadows of the flower bushes animals lay licking their chops, staring at the surreal beauty of the garden; hare and squirrel, deer and leopard, all in pairs, watching in silence.

Up in the trees the bright macaws and pigeon trafficked from branch to branch, not in a hurry for fruit and grain was in plenty.

They moved through the towering trees crawling with luxuriant creepers, with him ahead, occasionally stopping to acknowledge the nod of the animals with a flick of the ebony wand he carried in his hand. She followed close behind, watching the long bushy tail that peeked through the slit in his long greatcoat wag slowly left and right. It was amazing how light she felt underneath her arms as they trod with ease through the lush meadow and swamp; as if there was a crisp wind blowing underneath her wing.

They stopped on the crest of a little hill at the point where the rocky peak gave way suddenly, dipping down to the rolling valleys underneath. In the moon washed distance luxuriant fields of maize spread alongside *waru* and *ngwaci* vines, all well manured and watered, ripe for harvest. They merged with even more fields of wheat, millet and other grains that she had never seen, all lain in neat straight lines that spread far into the periphery. Looming up behind them, framed against the pale sky, the Alhaving's ivory-walled castle reached up towards the sky, the thin towers springing out of the high battlements stabbing the thin long strands of cloud like needles.

"Lovely, isn't it?" he said with that know-all smile playing on his moist lips, his arms spread out in an open gesture. "*Aaaah*! Paradise, my lady!" he cooed, a self-satisfied glint in his shiny yellow eyes. "The very finest that was ever made. And you know what?" he turned suddenly to face her, an open paw held towards her as he sunk slowly to one knee. "It can all be yours. Yes, *you* could own all this...right now, right here!"

He seemed pleased at the mesmerized look on her face.

"Yes, it can be all yours, to do with as you please. Now, *you* surely are not going to reject an offer like that, are you? Ah-ah!" he shook his head slowly, the stiff whiskers on his chin bristling. "Just imagine all those animals we passed down there bowing down to you as you pass, same to every blade of grass and the tiniest ant! The tide on the emerald seas will roll in to salute you, and the thunder booming in the hills will echo your name. Yes, this is all your world to play with, my dear, your world to command from atop this hill. And all that in exchange for what? A simple thing, my lady," he turned to her, the glimmer of the distant stars shining in his watery eyes. "Only by moving into the castle behind us with me, my lady- only that. Now, what do you say, my lovely?"

***

Njambi sprang out of bed and sank to her knees on the beat floor, her hands clutching at her moist face. Her breath whistled sharply through her clenched teeth as she clawed about in the dark for her little leather-bound Bible, that she usually kept by the bedside.

"Go away, *shetani*!" she whispered through clenched teeth, groping about on her hands and knees in the dark.

At the other end of the room her son stirred and turned over on the mat he shared with his sister, disturbed by the commotion. It was that hour of the night when all was still; the hour of the witches.

Chapter Fourteen

NDONGA lay on his back and gazed into the liquid darkness, which swam with hundreds of formless night creatures. He was unable to go to sleep because of the itching all over his neck and arms where the nappier grass blades had sliced his skin. There was a raspiness at the back of his throat that refused to go away and which occasionally induced a dry cough that left him gasping for breath. Sometimes it was so severe he would hear his mother turn over on the creaky bed, disturbed in her sleep, before settling back in her steady snore. He didn't know it, but it was the fine felt hairs on the leaves and stems of the nappier that he had inhaled all through the day, and which had settled there at the back of his throat. Working up phlegm and swallowing only made the place coarser. It was most uncomfortable.

Beside him on the mat they shared his little sister Mukami slept peacefully, her snoring soft and regular, angelic. Their mother had also engaged in a deeper snore on the bed.

Only Ndonga was awake, kept company by the scurrying of the rats and the scaly rasp of the cockroaches on the cooking utensils in the corner. In the stillness of the night, as usual his thoughts came back to haunt him, depriving him further of the sleep that he needed most to rest his tired limbs for yet another tiring day awaiting him at the crack of dawn.

It was now nine months since they had returned to the farm, and it was getting even more unbearable by the day. Their mother said that they had only one more month to go, and then they would complete repaying the debt his father had accrued in illness. But even that one month seemed like a year. That was because now things had changed for the worse. They now had to not only do more work, but also work under constant supervision.

Where Ndonga had had a fairly easy time picking coffee berries with the other children on the estate, now he had to cut nappier and alfalfa for the cattle and ensure they were well fed and watered. It was not as easy as he had anticipated when he had first agreed to take on the task. On top of that there was the tiring job of scraping dung in their pens and pushing it on the wheelbarrow to the manure pit. It was the most difficult task, and even as the days passed he still couldn't get the hang of that heavy wheelbarrow.

And yet he couldn't complain. His father's debts needed to be paid.

Going back to the coffee fields would mean less money, pushing the date of completion even further away.

It was at the manure pit where his mother's turn began. She turned the composting manure and wheeled it on to the cabbage and maize fields. That is, after she was done with washing in the kitchen yard and scrapping the giant urns in the smoky kitchen where the farmhands' porridge was prepared.

It was tough work indeed, pushing the heavy wheelbarrow laden with dung; but then it had to be done.

And to imagine that all the while there was always someone hovering in the vicinity, if not the farm owner or his wife, then it was one of the Maasai guards. And all of them were looking for the slightest excuse to cancel a day's wages.

Sometimes Juma came by from overseeing work at the coffee estate and helped push the wheelbarrow. But then he had to be careful because it was clear he was not expected to help in the cattle yard, save for only milking time. His work was out in the fields. The cattle *boma* had been under Yakobo's charge, and his widow had said with her own mouth that she would manage together with her child.

Only Mukami still had a fairly easy time working on the coffee estate as had been before. But still she now had to attain a set measure of berries a day to earn her wage, and so she couldn't afford to kid around. Indeed often she had to set out earlier and stay later than the other children.

But now Mother said there was only one more month to go. A measure of relief came over Ndonga at the prospect. He wished the day would come sooner when they would take their possessions and leave the farm. It was no longer the same as it had been when Father was around. He could no longer run down to the river to swim in the muddy water with the boys, or cast his home-made manila line with a flattened worm on the hook into the still depths for mudfish. Neither could he play ball any more. All the hours of the day he had to sweat it out in the cattle *boma*. And, boy, those cattle could really feed! No sooner had he put a ration in the trough than he would have to dash off with the wheelbarrow to fetch more fodder.

And then, just when he thought he was going to steal a break after all the feeding and cleaning it would be milking time...*Aah!* This was just too much!

As these thoughts coursed through Ndonga's mind he raised his hand to brush at a whining mosquito. The callused palm brushed his cheek, grazing a tender itchy cut that was inflaming into a welt. It felt like a brush from the stiff wire-brush that Kioko used to clean his files in the workshop. He winced and forced his hand to stay down. Scratching would only make the cuts worse.

It was as he lay thus that Ndonga heard noises outside, sounds like someone...no, some *people* moving stealthily about in the night. The movements, although measured, were different from the usual night sounds. Someone was no doubt stealing about the house.

Ndonga stiffened, his ears cocked. Beside him his little sister turned over and engaged into deeper breathing, pulling the patched blanket closer about her ears.

As his sense of alarm grew Ndonga thought he heard the sound of something pouring; like water coming out of a jerrycan. He rose to one elbow, puzzled.

He probably couldn't be making it all up in his dreams. The sounds were far too clear and distinct. Or could he?

He blinked twice rapidly, trying to clear his mind. Could it be one of the yellow jerrycans they used to store water that had tipped over?

Shortly after the thought came the smell of fuel came clearly to his nostrils. It was a familiar smell, the distinct smell of the fuel Juma often poured into the generator in the little hut beside the cattle *boma* whenever there was power failure at the farm. Ndonga listened, greatly perplexed, now certain that it was not his imagination playing tricks with him; because his eyes were dry as day.

That was before the night suddenly exploded in a bright orange flower that shot up skywards, enveloping the corner of the hut furthest from where they were sleeping. The enormous light, like a giant ball of sun that had ballooned out of the bowels of the earth, flooded the room through the chinks where the rotting boards in the wall had separated, hissing hungrily.

"*Mwaki!* ... *Mama! Fire!*" screamed Ndonga as he sprang to his feet, shaking his little sister with urgency, at the same time as he leapt onto the narrow bed where their mother slept.

The guards and other farmhands who worked in the kitchen yard rushed to the forlorn little hut by the cattle *boma*, roused from sleep by the yelling, punctuated by the dry crack of the hungry flames in the still night which were borne on the faint night breeze. Even those in Kampi Nyasi yonder saw the fire and rushed out to help, running through the darkened fields.

They fought the fire, dousing it with water that they drew from the drinking trough in the cattle shed.

As for the cattle, they gazed from the darkness of their pens with fright in their glassy unblinking eyes, tapping their hooves and mowing, startled at the bright flames that had suddenly lit up the night. They appeared ready to bolt into the night, save for the restraining barriers lowered in place at the entrances.

People ran helter-skelter, their terrified cries adding to the confusion, knocking into each other in the rush to put out the fire by whatever means, be it broken twigs, or spadefuls of earth hurled at the angry orange flower.

But it was all in vain.

The fire, aided by the explosion of the Chinese cooking stove, defied all their efforts and engulfed the little hut in a deadly embrace, the hungry flames lapping at the wilted tree branches that fought them as if in warning, finding welcome tinder in the timber and cardboard walls.

Soon the first soot-coloured zinc sheet curled up in the heat and disengaged from the harnessing capped nails with a soft pop. It flew into the night, wafting like a fiery flying saucer on the warm current created by the fire. It landed with a fiendish slowness in the nearby maize field.

The farmhands watched from a distance, aghast, their sooty palms held in fright in front of their shiny faces, unable to approach the fire because of the fierce heat. All their efforts were in vain.

In no time the little hut was reduced to charred rubble and smoldering embers.

Chapter Fifteen

NJAMBI was inconsolable. As it became apparent that the situation was not going to be put under control, she stood watching the fire slowly defy the efforts of the workers, her hands linked behind her head, the half-burnt branch she had been using to battle the flames abandoned at her feet. She was covered all over in ashes, and there was an angry blister on her forehead where a flying spark had caught her.

But the worst of the defeat was written in her eyes, which were pale and blank, ringed with hopelessness, her mouth dry, jaw hanging slack, utterly lost for words.

The few possessions they had salvaged were in the yard. Not much really. There was the burnt shell of the metal trunk, whose lid had flown open in the hurry to lug it out, spilling all the clothing. Beside the trunk were a few shoes, some with the soles burnt into twisted lumps of charred rubber. Yakobo's old wool coat rested atop the pile, one blackened sleeve smouldering, ready to fall off. Hardly any of the children's clothing was in a wearable state. Save for the folding chair that had miraculously survived, everything else had been licked black by the flames.

Looking at this miserable pile something suddenly snapped in Njambi and, running towards the group of women from the village who were ringed at one end of the yard, she demanded, "My children!...Where are my children you women?"

"Right here. They are safe," said someone at the back of the gathering.

"*Where*?" demanded Njambi, a ring of hysteria in her voice.

"Over here, Mama Ndonga!" Someone tried to guide her to the spot where the children were seated watched over by the women.

And then all of a sudden she broke loose, her clawed fingers tearing at her disarrayed hair, the *lesso* cloth tied around her waist flying loose behind her. "*Wuuuuuuiiiii...!*" Her long-drawn wail shattered the stunned silence that had settled over the gathering, echoing through the grey night. "Someone toss me a rope...Toss me a rope, someone! ...I will finish it all off! ...*Wuuuui...Ngai- Ngai!*"

Before anyone could stop her she tore across the yard into the maize field, beating her breast, eyes rolling white, her head tossing back and forth like a person in a trance.

"Quick, someone catch her!" called one of the men.

Two young men dashed after her, sprinting as fast as they could. For a while the three crashed through the maize plantation, the woman yelling at the top of her voice. But her younger pursuers were good runners, easily gaining on her. It was after a long winding chase that they finally managed to wrestle her to the ground.

Even with her seized hands locked firmly behind her, it was still a struggle for the young men getting her back.

And as she collapsed on the ground, her palms beating at the earth, the women gathered around, trying to calm her.

It took Mama Pima's bear hug to hold her still, and lengthy soothing words to get her to cease her hysterical babbling.

It was starting to get light in the eastern sky when she was eventually led off to Kampi Nyasi to rest in the house of one of the women, her tear-stained children herded behind her, wrapped in the worn coats and *lessos* that some of the farmhands had donated.

Chapter Sixteen

NJAMBI heaved on the wheelbarrow and felt a muscle in her back rip. The barrow wouldn't move. It was stuck in a rut in the muddy path, the dark mud thick and unyielding. "*Ngai*!" she lamented, wiping sweat from her brow. She gave another heave, putting in more effort, and the barrow tilted to the side, careening out of her grip, spilling the load of dung in the mud.

She felt the earth come up to meet her, the hot afternoon sun burning the back of her scalp. She let go of the barrow handle and sunk to her knees by the pathside.

Visions of the farm-owner played in her mind like a stuck record, the words he had kept reminding her as the *fundi* build the lean-to by the chicken house, where they would now have to live on borrowed items and time, refusing to go away.

"...You burnt down my house, woman...my house! All my materials...timber, iron sheets, all destroyed... *burnt*!

You are given housing, for which you don't have to pay a cent in rent; and yet you turn around and burn down the very house! What indolence! God alone knows what would have happened had the cattle *boma* caught fire...Thanks to the quick action of the guards it didn't. We probably would be speaking thousands here, woman ...millions of shillings lost! ...Thank God it was only your house, you *jinga* woman!"

"But it was not her fault...she didn't start the fire..." someone in the gathering had tried to defend her.

141

To which the irate farm-owner had thundered, "Shut up, you fool. *Nyamaza*! You don't know half the measure of loss we would be talking now, you hear? *You* wouldn't know. All that you stupid people know is *shamba* work, and stealing from me, that is about all! Do you know what it costs to put up a single structure of these buildings standing on the farm? Eh? Do you? ...*Jinga sana*! I bet you wouldn't even know what a dog's kennel costs!"

In the ensuing lull JP had paced around, fists punching the air, seething with rage.

"And now you will have to pay for the damage... yes, you will pay for all my iron sheets and timber that you destroyed, you *jinga* woman!" he had announced at the end of his pacing. "You must pay for every single thing that was destroyed in the fire!"

"But this was just salvaged bits of rotten wood and rusty scrap metal that no one had use for, so how can I pay for it?" Njambi had protested, rage burning inside her, hardly believing what she was hearing.

"Shut up!" he had whirled around, glowering at her. "*You* will pay for every little thing you destroyed, woman!" he had stated flatly, stabbing a finger into her face, bloodshot eyes glinting menacingly. "You will pay; there is no question about that. Understand?"

As the picture of the irate farm-owner replayed in her mind, Njambi, resting on her haunches in the dirt, leaned forward and buried her face in her rough hands. Tears of frustration welled in her eyes at the prospect of another six months work on the farm to pay for the damage; and the humiliation of having to beg for even the clothes she wore.

And as she thought about these things, the pounding headache that had been her unwelcome companion lately started again, threatening to split her scalp right in two.

That was until she felt the clammy little palm of her son resting on her shoulder. "Mama...Mama! Are you alright?"

Ndonga looked more of an eighteen-year-old street ruffian now, his bony frame angled forward, shoulders stooped, long arms bent at the elbows as if perpetually in readiness to lug something. His cheek bones stuck out more now, the skin across his brow stretched tight with worry, and in the shadows beneath the sweat-slicked eyebrows his eyes had attained the pale focus of a man who works like a mule, but who must still worry about keeping his measly job. This life was taking a heavy toll on him.

Having waited for his mother to return the wheelbarrow in vain Ndonga had got worried. He decided to come and investigate.

Lately she had appeared rather ill, even though she insisted she was fine. She was growing even gaunter of appearance, her brow lined with constant worry.

"Mama! Here...let me help you. You *must* go and rest," he breathed close to her ear as he struggled to get her to her feet. Njambi recognized the bony frame of her son and willed herself to rise to her feet and help him get her out of the mud. She had to lean heavily on him all the same, for she was very weak.

But still, even in her distress, she had to smile at the strength of her son, who had been just a wee bit of a boy the other day. For a twelve-year-old, it amazed her sometimes what an ox of a lad he had transformed into...so strong, this Ndonga of hers...

As son led his mother staggery step by step to the

little lean-to at the back of the chicken house where they lived, a pair of eyes was watching.

Juma had been on his way to the store to collect a piece of hose to fix a burst section of the spraying network that spanned the coffee estate when he chanced on the scene.

Watching the boy lead his mother slowly to the shack, bravely taking up most of her weight as they struggled along, Juma felt anger claw at his inside. It was so intense and sudden, welling up inside him like warm bile from an upset stomach. Then it was gone, and in its wake confusion remained. And as the two limped slowly round the corner, Juma turned and went into the tool store, troubled by thoughts.

He pitied the widow, and at the same time he felt anger. He wanted to help, and yet he realized- with a tinge of shame- that there didn't seem much he could do to help. Or was there?

Say, what if JP conceded to their leaving the farm, where then would they go? Were they assured of finding work elsewhere? Or would they turn into street beggars like those who sit at street corners in Kiambu town singing church hymns and shoving chipped enamel bowls at passersby? The picture of Yakobo and his wife on that very first day when he had found them in the trees was still clear in his mind. The helplessness and glaring want was all too visible on the two; as if there could be no worse fate than the one they were fleeing from. This was one picture that had refused to go out of his mind's eye even with the passing of the years.

What support, if any, could he offer the widow and the children if they were to be allowed to leave the farm?

Now, that was a tough one. For starters, it occurred to him that he had no savings to speak of. All these years he had been working on the farm, and yet he didn't even have a house of his own in his home village. Neither did he have any social support to fall back on incase he hit on hard times. All these years he had been living like a bird that perches where the night finds it, blowing away the little money he had been earning, first treating a chest infection the previous year more or less similar to his friend Yakobo's affliction. He remembered the doctors telling him the very same thing they had told Yakobo, and him wondering at the time if it was only a ploy to get him to pay up for the drugs. Indeed, just like Yakobo, the doctor had warned him to stop working with farm chemicals unless he had proper protective gear; something he had found most absurd.

The rest of his money he had blown away one way or the other in the pleasure halls of Kampi Nyasi.

At this point in his line of thought the picture of his friend Yakobo came back clearly to him. It was that of him on that evening after they had finished measuring his new house. Yakobo had raised these concerns as they walked off to Mama Pima's, and as usual Juma had been non-committal, preferring to shrug it all away. Looking back, he realized that Yakobo had probably had a point, scary though it had been at the time.

All the same, even as Juma pondered this, he couldn't help wondering what had come of JP.

While the man had never been known to be the most generous of people, Juma had never seen him go to such lengths to recover a debt all the years he had been working on the farm. Often, when it became apparent he wasn't going to get what he wanted he would simply have the man hauled off to the local Police station and have the boys kick some sense into him for two days or so and then let him go. That was JP's style, and it was always effective enough to put the fear of God in any prospective tricksters. But for this...

It made one wonder just how much money the man had lent Yakobo...Or *had* he...?

As he pondered over this new thought, Juma realized that there had been no one to witness the man give Yakobo the money as he claimed. It even came as a surprise to Njambi to learn that Yakobo had been given a loan. Meaning that, as matters stood now, it was a pact made with the dead...who was not there to speak for himself.

And so, the question that begged was, was it right to seek redress from the dead?...

Even as Juma mulled over this matter, he realized that the burning of the house had further compounded it. Now, *that* complicated matters. And JP was demanding compensation for destruction of his property- what absurdity!

Juma felt anger well up inside him as he came to this point. Just what right had JP to demand payment for such a shack as that? Just what was the man made of inside? Wasn't there an iota of humanity? Just how heartless could one get...? Such a shack as that, fashioned out of rotting wood that he didn't even have use for...It was sheer absurdity!

With his fist clenched in a fit of anger that he had never experienced before Juma forced himself to break from his winding train of thought and walk towards the store.

But still the thoughts followed him even as he walked away, refusing to give him rest.

For some reason too much seemed to have happened too soon...somehow it didn't add up.

Yakobo's family had been living all this while in that little house, and there had never been a fire; even when the children had been crawling around as they learnt how to walk. Ndonga, for instance, had been the most likely to have started a fire in his day, given his development had been the most troublesome.

Why now?

And that was just the tinder to spark a volatile situation. The rest of the farmhands, forgetting for a while their everyday complaints about work on the farm, were beginning to talk about the matter. Juma could hear them whisper among themselves in discreet little gatherings, hushing up whenever he approached. It was apparent they were unhappy about the treatment JP was subjecting Yakobo's widow to.

Just that morning Juma had had to break up a heated discussion outside the tool shed and urge Wangari, the portly loud-mouth, to break it off and everyone to hurry to their work places.

But even as they went, dragging their feet as if not in any hurry to disperse, he could see the way they eyed Njambi as she emerged from the maize field and entered the store followed by her children. There was a sense of unease every time the woman passed by a gathering.

The farmhands watched in silence as Yakobo's little girl clambered up coffee trees, popping berries into her tin from daybreak to sundown, and were in agreement that the family were being unfairly harassed. And it was the stone silence with which they answered Juma's orders to return to work that frightened him most. Their vacant eyes no longer portrayed fear.

Take that Wangari for one. A stump-like midget of a woman, she was a cheerleader of sorts, who was openly defiant in her rather loud gossip with the other women around her as they worked along the rows. Her comments on the situation of Yakobo's widow were blunt and unflattering, and she never cared to look over her shoulder to see if anyone was passing.

Juma feared that with people like Wangari- who for her size wielded surprising clout among the women- stoking up the anger; very soon there might be trouble. For only a worker understands best another's plight. Weren't they cast out of the same mold?

As Juma slung the piece of hose over his shoulder and locked up the store, he decided to pass by the little lean-to and check on Njambi. She had appeared to be in a rather bad state as her son assisted her to her feet.

Njambi, reclining on the narrow bed, was a pitiable sight, her shoulders sticking up through her thinning dress as she gasped in an effort to swing her legs onto the bed, her moist face quivering in the effort. Unlike on other days, this time round there was no warm smile on her face at the sight of the visitor. As Ndonga hurried round to tuck her legs in, Juma slowly walked up to the side of the bed and, kneeling, felt her brow.

"How are you feeling, Mama Ndonga?"

It was an effort for her to open her eyes, and even harder to speak. On recognizing him she gave a weak smile. "I am fine, Juma. I will be okay," she croaked.

"I see. Still, you don't look half fine to me. You must be thirsty too." He walked over to the water jerrican by the hearth and poured her a tub of water. Supporting her head with his arm he made her drink. She took two gulps of the water, swallowing with effort, and licked her dry lips, gasping for air. He made her drink a little more, and then lay her back on the beddings. Wetting a rag he dabbed it slowly on her moist brow.

"Have you anything for her to eat?" he said to the scared boy, who was standing by, his eyes darting wildly, uncertain of what to do next.

Ndonga foraged in the pans piled on the rack by the hearth and found some mashed food in one of the sooty pots, which he ladled onto an enamel plate and brought over.

They had to give up after the second spoonful when it became apparent Njambi desired being left alone to rest.

"You stay in here and watch over her, you hear?" said Juma to the boy. "I'll go down to the farm and see if I can find someone to take over at the cattle yard. I'll be back in a while after she has rested. We need to take her down to the clinic to have her examined.

Meanwhile try and feed her some of that food, okay?" The boy nodded, his eyes wide with worry. "She must try to eat something. She will be well enough in a while, I am certain. It is probably just fatigue."

Having seen to it that she was well tucked in bed Juma was preparing to leave when from the corner of his eye he saw the door of the little lean-to swing inwards. It opened an inch and the well-polished calf-leather toe of JP's unmistakable shoe stepped over the threshold.

Juma looked up slowly, and locked eyes with the cold stare of the farm-owner.

Unknown to him JP, having just had his lunch, had been watching the movements of his storekeeper from the rooftop terrace, which accorded him a clear view of most of the farm.

"And the coffee picking is going on just fine while you take time off to visit your *gacungwa*, is it, Juma?" JP's tone, just like his stare, was icy, knife-like. "*Ehe?* Is this all the work you people do for the afternoon when I am not around?"

"Er...Mama Ndonga has been taken ill, *Mzee*...And I only came by to check on her."

JP's gaze now shifted beyond the startled storekeeper into the darkness of the hut. He took in the woman, white-eyed, lying stiffly on the bed. Her son stood fidgeting nervously besides.

"And there are all three of you just idling in here!" an angry gurgling noise sounded deep in his throat, his moist face darkening. "Ndonga! *Out!*" he bellowed suddenly, sweeping into the room like an elephant in a cage of twigs. "I am not going to pay you people for lazing around doing nothing on the farm, hear?" A speck of foam had appeared at the corner of his mouth as his face crumbled in anger. "I am fed up with this nonsense about illness every other day! Get out, you *chokora* ...get back to your work!"

Ndonga, who had been searching for an opening in the crowded doorway, slipped past the rotund farm-owner and out of the hut.

"*Jinga sana!*" added JP after him, taking a swing at his backside with his shoe.

"As for you," he turned to Juma, who was standing stiffly in the middle of the room, wringing his hands. "Who told you your responsibilities included seeing to the health of the workers, eh? Who gave you the power to decide who works and who doesn't...tell me!"

"I only felt it my duty..."

"*Nyamaza*! Shut up!" JP was really worked up. "You think you are very smart, eh? Tell me, what are the people in the clinic down by the factory doing, Eh? What is their job- do you know, you dung-brained fool? Eh? Did you take her there, if indeed she was ill as you say?" JP fumed, edging towards him.

As Juma retreated, at a loss for words with which to defend himself, he knew it would only take a single utterance to set the man's full wrath pouring on him.

"Get out, you dog! I pay you to ensure the coffee is picked and not to mind if some hapless widow is well or not, hear? Get out...*Ngui*!"

The thoroughly humiliated Juma collected his coiled hose left by the entrance and bowed out of the hut, hastening down the path that led through the maize field.

And it was just as good he had not answered back, for, hovering outside the hut within hearing distance pretending to patrol the chicken yard was one of the Maasai guards. Somehow, of late they were always within a shouting distance, hounding their employer wherever he went, ready to do his bidding.

Njambi, now that she was alone in the hut with her worked-up employer, drew back on the narrow bed and started to rise, frightened all of a sudden.

After the others had taken leave the hut had become too still, the air charged.

"He-he-heeeee...!" JP's manic laugh suddenly shattered the electric silence. "Unwell, eh? Woman?" He was standing above her, watching her keenly, eyes roving slowly all over her. In the darkness of the hut they radiated a reddish glow, bright and feral, like a bat's. They brought back the unearthly image she had visualized in her dream just the day before, the illusion so vivid and real in the gloom of the hut. "Unwell, eh?, waYakobo?" he moved around the bed, inspecting her. "Well, there's a way to find out, you know…"

His tone, now that they were alone, had changed, a huskiness replacing the sharpness that had been in it. All of a sudden the fear became real. Mama Ndonga, her illness forgotten, suddenly wished she had left the hut while she still could. She could hardly see him in the gloom in the hut. He had kicked the door shut, cutting out the light.

Still she could feel his presence strong in the enclosed space, his breath measured, like that of a cat stalking prey. And in the deadly intimacy of predator and prey she could feel every turn of his plotting mind.

"Unwell, eh?, proud woman?…. Heh…heh!" he laughed softly, coming round to peer at her face. His teeth shone white, the profile of his moist face zooming in and out of her focus. "You know what? I don't believe you."

He reached out to touch her arm, but she brushed his hand away.

"Aha! And frightened you are too,…he-heh!"

He continued the circling game for a while, measuring her, evaluating her strengths, piecing out the weak links where the chain would snap.

And then suddenly he closed the gap between them, grabbing her by the collar of her dress, just as she started to rise off the bed. "And I see you remember well the humiliation you subjected me to that day long ago…"

There was a flash of white in the darkness as a

self-satisfied sneer spread slowly on the farm-owner's face.

"He-He-He-Heeeee...!" he laughed in that strange way, his eyes glowing with malicious intent. "Tell you what, waYakobo; I have waited for so long. I have played the game with you all this while, patiently hoping you would come to your senses, woman. But now I think my patience runs dry. It seems to me like you are never going to give in to me, he-he-heeee....!"

He raised a hand and wiped the moisture off his brow.

"Yes, you have humiliated me for so long. And all the while there was little I could do. But you know what? Now he is no longer here, woman—he is dead...gone...! And perhaps it is now time we settled this once and for all...yes, we must settle this little matter now," he said softly, swallowing in the semi-dark. "And for this once, *you* are going to do exactly as I say!" His breathing was harsh and paced in the heightened silence following the pronouncement, his face glistening with the mounting excitement. "And you know what, woman? I think I like you even more when you look this way- frightened and helpless. You excite me...he-heee!" he laughed softly, gasping, even as his hands groped about in the air, measuring.

Njambi opened her mouth to scream, visions of that rainy evening long ago replaying in her mind with a fresh vividness. The vision of JP looming above her, the baby sleeping on the bed besides, as the rain drummed steadily on the roof, effectively trapping Yakobo and Ndonga out in the cattle yard where they had gone to attend to an emergency.

She had not dared share the incident with Yakobo for fear of the resultant repercussions. And all this while she had thought it over, forgotten. But how wrong she had been...

"Yes, you remember, do you?" said JP, his face close to hers in the darkness, shiny little eyes boring into hers. "Remember this?" he whipped around his wrist, which he had bared, and showed her the scar that was still embedded in his skin, and which had been inflicted by her teeth as she fought him off. That was before her husband's whistling had sounded outside as he returned from the emergency in the cattle shed, interrupting them. In Yakobo's naivety nothing had seemed amiss, and she had kept her lips closed.

"Aha! Indeed you do! Remember the day you slammed the door in my face? Eh, woman? Remember that night? You humiliated me, of all people, on my own farm! Remember I promised you I would be back?" The simmering in the depths of his gaze was like molten lava down a volcano shaft. "Well, now the day has come."

Such fear as she had never known took hold of her, constricting her throat like a vice. Yet again she opened her mouth to scream.

"Ha-Ha-Haaaa...! Why don't you just save your breath, proud woman?" His voice was thick with coarse derision, the summative words grating in the tense closeness, like the rasp of sandpaper on grainy wood. "You will achieve nothing shouting at the top of your voice, woman. No one will hear you. And even if they do there is absolutely nothing they can do." He started undoing the buckle of his shiny snakeskin belt. "I have two guards out there with instructions to deal *ruthlessly* with anyone who approaches this house. There is just no way out. See? You are all mine now,

woman.... To do with as I please...He-he-heeee...!"
he finished with a soft laugh that echoed within the
narrow confines of the little cardboard shack.

The manic glint in his eye was frightening as he
crowded over her on the bed, grabbing for the front
of her bodice. She gasped and drew back against
the timber wall, causing the fabric to rip, leaving her
breasts bared to his absorbing scrutiny. "Aah! And
they still have the bewitching ripeness," he said in a
passion-filled whisper, beholding one of the cupped
breasts. "You don't know how many nights I have
visualized you in my sleep, woman, wishing you
would come to me. You don't know how I've longed
to touch your breast...just like that child. They were
far much fuller and rounded then when you were
breastfeeding," he said in a captivated boyish voice,
peering closer at her in the dim light. "I wish I'd had
the chance to have you then. How so sweet it would
have felt against my hand...!" There was a far-away
look on his moist face now that was almost pained.

"*Don't!*" she snapped suddenly as he reached to
touch, slapping away his hand. "Don't touch me, you
evil man!"

"Aha! You want to play the seducing game now,
do you?" He stepped back, a boyish grin on his face.
"I told you already that I have waited enough. Indeed
you must have thought that you had seen the last
of me when you slammed the door in my face that
night. Well, how wrong you were. No one escapes
JP, woman. *You* should know by now," he whispered
passionately, making another grab for her left breast.
As he inched closer his breath smoldered her face,
slobbery lips wetting her cheek. "*I* can be very patient,
you know."

He leaned above her, crowding her against the wall, a nervous smile playing on his face. He reached out and touched her trembling shoulder, his hand lingering a while to feel the warmth of her sweaty skin. She cringed back against the wall, slapping the hand away, her teeth bared in warning.

"Hey...hey, waYakobo, you know it doesn't have to be this way," he said more softly, changing tact. He settled beside her on the narrow bed, causing the termite-infested wood to squeak in protest. "You really don't have to fight me at all, Njambi. We can be good to each other, you know. Eh? What do you say?"

Njambi cringed further back against the wall, gazing steadily into his little eyes. She recalled the stories she had heard about the man. The vision of the owner of all the wealth of the world, the all powerful, that had played in her dreams shadowed over her thoughts. The one man who was capable of everything and anything- the Alhaving; and who could grant it or take it away at will.

For a while her gaze shifted from those flaming eyes, searching the bed for something with which to defend herself.

"Hey...hey, waYakobo. You are not planning to bash my head in with a plank now, are you?" He laughed in that demented manner, peering into her eyes. "You know, you don't really have to be so frightened of me," he cooed in that soft seductive voice he employed on an enthralled gathering around a rally dais, his afore hard face mellowing. "You know you are truly a beautiful woman, waYakobo, yes, ve-ery beautiful." He reached to touch her face in a caress. Yet again she brushed it aside.

"Now, now, Njambi, that is surely not the way

to act with a man who cares deeply for you, is it? Remember what I told you?" In the darkness of the hut his moist face brightened, eyebrows lifting in the manner of a boy who was in the know of something he was certain would blow the mind of the pastor's little girl away. "Remember what I said, Njambi? I, JP, can make life very beautiful for you. Yes, I can make it *ve-ery* beautiful! Think about it, I can order a government Mercedes just like the one Njeri uses to be at your service, complete with a chauffeur to take you wherever you want. I can put your children in the finest schools and build you a fine stone house... on a piece of land that you will choose from the many farmlands I own. You won't need to break a sweat in the fields at all! All the food you may need in this world will be brought right to where you are seated by servants- hundreds of them! Think about it...I can make your life very comfortable, woman." He got down on his knees beside the bed and grabbed for her hands, his face inching towards her lap. There was an expression on his face that begged almost desperately to be believed. "I, JP, have all the money in the world, you know...You only need to say the word, and I will have it granted. Come on, think about it. This needs to be only between you and I—we can forget the past and start a new future together..."

Seeing that the woman was still, JP took it for an invitation and reached to touch her, more confident this time, going for her enchanting breast that pushed against the thin fabric of her torn dress.

Without warning Njambi's arm shot up. She struck him hard on the wrist. "*Tigana nake, wee...* go away, you nasty man!" she snarled, fear rending her voice into a charged whisper. "I am still a married woman, and will never be your mistress, hear? *Don't* you touch me!"

JP, a little surprised, stepped back, massaging his stinging wrist. That is shortly before something snapped deep inside him. In that moment of enlightenment he seemed to remember who he was; JP, the feared political operator and millionaire farmer and businessman who's path no one dared cross.

"Mama Ndonga, are you going to be difficult still?" he snarled, climbing onto the bed. "I thought time had taught you a few lessons...eh? Remember this?" he fumed, pushing the scar on his arm into her face. "Eh? You have been like a spitting snake, throwing your indolence in my face all this while. Now I think it is time you got some of it back...yes, you leave me with little option!"

Straddling her, he halted her attempt to rise, knocking her back against the wall with a beefy forearm. His hand, no longer gentle, went for the hem of her dress, his massive weight pinning her down. A vicious slap across the face stilled her struggles.

Chapter Seventeen

NDONGA heaved on the laden wheelbarrow one last time, and as it rolled to a stop beside the chaff-cutter, he let out his breath in a tortured gasp. It had been hard cutting and gathering the nappier in the hot afternoon sun, but getting it up to the cattle shed on the heavy barrow was simply torture.

And as he regained his breath, dark face moist with the effort, he remembered the encounter with the farm-owner just a while back, and hastened to flick on the switch that operated the electric chaff-cutter.

Inside the sheds besides the cattle started lowing softly in anticipation of the feed.

As the machine hummed on, Ndonga lifted a bunch of nappier and placed it on the jutting spout, feeding it into the belly of the machine slowly like he had seen his father do countless times. This was the enjoyable part of the job, quite unlike the arduous cutting and gathering of the razor-edged grass, not to mention wheeling it up the slope. He stepped back, taking the opportunity to stretch his stiff back and wipe at the sweat on his brow, which had a bite like pepper whenever it seeped into a new cut the grass blades had opened in his skin.

He watched the huge wheels in the belly of the machine turn slowly, drawing in the nappier inch by inch, chopping it to little pieces that it ejected at the other end into the large wooden trough. It was amazing how the machine could reduce a whole barrow-full of fodder to just a tiny hill of chopped feed in such a short while.

As Ndonga fed the insatiable machine, his thoughts wandered back to his mother, lying there in the little ramshackle hut. He wondered how she was, and if the rest had made her feel better.

He dreaded the thought that the illness had got worse. It scared him, thinking of her writhing helplessly in the bed all alone, just like Father had been in his last days. Oh, it had been hell.

But still, how could it have happened to Father, of all people? This was the part he could not understand. There were other people who were better placed to die. That old hunchback who tended to the drying racks down by the factory for one; he was so old his eyes were almost lost in the folds of his wrinkled skin, almost all the teeth fallen out. Why couldn't it have been that one instead?

Rack his mind as he did he still couldn't come to terms with the fact that his father was indeed dead. He still had this strong conviction that the man had just gone for a walk, and that one day he would appear down the path in the maize field, a long fat sugarcane slung on his shoulder, a jolly whistle on his lips... just like in the olden days. Or it would be a drizzly evening and he would appear with Juma on the way from having a drink at Kampi Nyasi, the two telling his mother they were hungry for some of her mashed pot-made *irio*, laughing. Yes, Father was just going to pull a surprise one sunny Sunday afternoon, that was for sure.

All the same, he was glad somehow that his sister had not been with them at the time of their father's agony. It was good that she had been working out in the coffee estate. Otherwise there easily would have been two cases to worry about.

He worried a lot about little Mukami. He hoped the work over at the coffee estate was not as tiring as tending the cattle was.

Meanwhile, as the boy's thoughts wandered, the machine ate up the fodder inch by inch, the turning steel gears drawing in the leaf ends sticking out into the feeding spout, and onto which the boy was still holding. That was until Ndonga felt a tightening pull on the ends of his finger. The tightness turned to a tingling at his fingertips, like tiny pins probing under his fingernails. The next minute a searing heat was traveling up his hand.

Jerked back to the present Ndonga looked down at the humming machine, only to see his hand disappear into the narrow opening.

Panicking, he gave a tug, at the same time as he piped a piercing scream, striking feebly at the cutter manifold with his palm.

But the machine only hummed on, indifferent to his efforts, the numbing pain jolting up his weakening arm.

***

Juma had just got to the coffee estate when he realized he had forgotten to fetch a length of pvc piping that he would need to join the pieces of rubber hose. And so he turned and made his way back to the store, making a detour through the maize field. He was not ready for another encounter with JP after what had happened at Mama Ndonga's house.

It was as he was passing behind the cattle shed along the narrow track that circled the back of the tool shed that he heard the scream.

He ran round to the yard in front of the cattle pens, dropping the coiled hose he had been carrying.

When he saw the boy struggling with the humming machine the first thing that came to mind was turning off the power. He dashed to the master switch and snapped the main switch off, grinding all activity in the yard to a stop.

Chapter Eighteen

THEY crowded around the still boy resting in the shade, horrified at the messy pulp that his hand had been reduced to, and which he cradled in his lap.

Ndonga was shaking with the aftershock, his white eyes gazing vacantly at the muddy feet of the farm workers encircling him, face pale. Everyone was craning to see the injury, crowding him, and cutting out the fresh air he needed most.

There were the Maasai guards, who had got there first, together with the other farmhands from the kitchen yard. There was also the boy's shocked mother, who looked pale and distraught, being held by two women. They all seemed uncertain what to do.

JP came around shortly from the direction of the chicken-house. There was a look of confusion on his moist face. As he hurried along in his shambly walk he tucked his hanging shirt into the band of his trouser, pausing to wipe the moisture on his face.

"What are you all crowding around the boy for?" he demanded, eyeing the wary crowd. "Can't you see he needs air? Eh? Or are you too thick in the head? ... Siara! Sempei!" he called to the guards.

"*Epa, Mzee!*" said the guards, springing forward.

"Get these people back to work...*Haraka*! They have little business doing here anyway."

The crowd, on seeing the guards approach, scattered and grudgingly backed away.

Mixed emotions played on the farm-owner's face as he examined the boy's injury. Leaning against a tree close by, still watched over by the two women, the

163

boy's mother sat with her hands in her lap, her dress hanging askew at the bust where a number of buttons had popped out. She was speechless with shock.

His mind still whirring JP shambled off, ordering Juma to prepare the boy as he went to fetch the car.

The Range Rover came around shortly and they carried the by then moaning boy inside, placing him on a plastic sheeting that had been hastily spread on the backseat to avoid soiling the fabric.

Juma climbed in after the boy. JP and his bodyguard got into the front. As for the mother, who had shortly slipped into a faint in the arms of the restraining women, mumbling incomprehensible words, she had to be carried off to her shack behind the chicken-house and put to bed.

As the Range Rover swung out of the yard, churning up dirt, the Maasai guards moved menacingly towards the growing gathering of workers. Reluctantly they dispersed, discussing the matter in pairs as they went.

***

Miss Julia Nyokabi had suffered an equally restless morning. She had woken up with a splitting headache that had assailed her all through the night.

Shrugging off the thought of calling her business partner and getting him to take up her cases for the day she had set out for the office as usual. Such was her attachment to Nyokabi&K'Opiyo Co. Advocates, the firm she had co-founded four years back she could not afford to stay away for a day because of a headache. And it was not to say her law practice had been a disappointment either. Far from it.

In the past six years she had been in practice her stature had been on a steady upward rise, thanks to her dogged determination to make a success of herself and the brilliance she had exhibited in the courtroom.

Indeed such was her keenness her fellows on the bar had nicknamed her 'Lady Wasp', a title she carried with unapologetic pride. They took immense pleasure in slinging epithets at her at the end of a spitting session from which she almost always emerged victorious. For Miss Nyokabi stung just like a wasp guarding a nest!

Her nest had acquired quite some padding over the years too, thanks to the line of corporate clients she had on her waiting list, and who entrusted their legal affairs with her. Indeed it was one such client that she had business with today, and that was partly the reason why she couldn't allow the headache to keep her in bed.

Well, brilliant Miss Nyokabi might be in her line of business, but then matters of the body- as the doctor would say- tend to have little respect for such when they go berserk. This she soon realized. And it was with the increasing migraine that she was forced to cut short an interview with her client and telephone a cab to take her to her doctor at Kikuyu Hospital. Yes, the body could be such an ass sometimes.

An hour later she sat in the hospital waiting room watching the grainy TV picture, waiting for the medication she had been given to quit playing games with her vision. She was digesting the doctor's caution to slow down on her work schedule and even think about taking a holiday somewhere to ease the stress. There was the suggestion to visit her married sister in Botswana.

Well, that would certainly be a welcome idea. Getting to catch up with her nieces' progress would certainly be uplifting, seeing as the old family house was getting too lonesome now that Mom and Pop were no longer here to chat with in the evenings over *tangawizi* tea.

Really what the lawyer was doing in the hospital waiting room, eyes fixed on a TV she wasn't conscious of was procrastinating over the matter. She was trying to make up her mind whether to go home to bed or defy the doctor and go back to work.

Her thoughts were interrupted by the entry of an injured boy, who was cradling his bloodied hand close to his chest, whimpering softly. He was flanked by the two men accompanying him, one beefy and well fed and the other quite the opposite, scrawny and lean. It was the frightened look on the boy's face that caught the lawyer's attention though. No doubt the injury was serious, judging from the look on his face, even as he tried to brave the pain.

She watched as the boy was led to the admission desk, wondering what might have caused the injury, and just how serious it was.

Fighting the wave of nausea Miss Nyokabi rose and approached one of the men who had brought in the boy.

"*Jambo!*" she said to the burly man, putting on her best smile despite the pulsing migraine. "The boy's injury seems serious." She jerked her thumb at the swinging doors through which the patient had been taken.

The man stopped pacing and turned around slowly, an unfriendly look on his moist face. "*Eee,*" he said gruffly, watching her through slitted eyes. "Rather serious."

"What caused the injury, do you know?" said the lawyer, getting a little curious from the man's manner.

"'Don't know," snapped the man. "Maybe you should ask him, woman." He seemed a familiar face, although with her reawakening headache she couldn't quite place him.

"The hand appeared crushed. Must have been quite painful," persisted the lawyer, not about to be dissuaded.

"Look, young woman, will you mind your own business!" was the smug reply that was hurled at her, the moist face no longer civil.

Outside in the parking lot the impatient taxi driver, who was watching the waiting area, gave a blast of the horn, eager to get back to some other business.

"Well, if you so say," said Miss Nyokabi, turning back to the bench where she had left her medication in a brown envelope. "It really is none of my business, I suppose. In any case I've got this splitting headache to worry about. Have a nice day!" She amused herself with the parting shot she liked to confer on lawyers in the courtroom who were yet to see the finest side of her.

Nevertheless as the cab backed off the kerb and turned on the loose gravel the picture of the boy cradling the bloodied arm lingered in her mind, the scared look on his face haunting her.

It must be her line of business that made her unnecessarily curious about other people's affairs, she told herself as the undulating countryside rolled past outside the car window. It probably would be gone by the time she woke from an hour's rest in her bed.

***

The trouble at the farm started rather unexpectedly. Wangari, the fat loud-mouth, walked up in the stifling midday heat and dumped her sack-load on the dusty floor of the collection shed, where a few other women were resting after delivering their loads. Whipping up the edge of her worn *lesso* cloth she wiped at the sweat on her rounded face and sat down on the sack with a sigh. "I think I just had enough of this farm...I am quitting!" she announced in her accustomed high piercing voice.

"*Heeei*! I have heard that line too often!" said someone lounging on her sack against one of the thick posts holding up the roof, waving her hand dismissively. "Please let me enjoy my break in peace, Wangari." The accomplice seated beside her laughed.

"It is true, don't you two laugh!" said Wangari seriously, bending to wipe her brow with the edge of her tightly-wound old *lesso* cloth that had dried blackjack seeds clinging to it.

"Why are you leaving, Wangari?" said one of the women by name waMurage, who had a thin long face that was wrinkled and darkened by sunburn.

"Ah! I am just tired. I hardly see what I get out of all this sweating in the sun!" said the stout woman, spreading her *lesso* on the ground. "I have worked far too hard here for too little."

"Just that? I thought someone had wronged you."

"I am really leaving, I tell you. Why? Look at me, waMurage -I am always in debt!"

"But we all are- I mean, look around you, Wangari. Who among these women seated around you doesn't owe someone money? Eh? Who doesn't have problems?"

"Indeed. Take me, for instance," said a little grey-haired woman named Nyakiambi, springing to her feet. She was still surprisingly nimble for her age. "I owe the grocer a hundred shillings worth of *sukuma* and tomatoes, the shopkeeper over a hundred and fifty in goods taken on credit...not to mention the dressmaker in the village. She said she is not going to release my white church dress until I settle with her. Ah! I have so many debts to settle!"

"Only three hundred shillings is what you call a debt?" said a gangly woman at the far end named Njunge. "I say, you don't know what a debt is, woman!"

"Tell her, Njunge!" encouraged someone with a laugh.

"I personally am running debts totaling over a thousand and a half...a *thousand*...And you would hardly tell. And yet they keep on piling every day. It bothers me, is true, but then it doesn't stop the sun rising in the east and setting in the west. And I don't regret that I owe so many people such a huge sum of money- no, I don't. And I will pile up even more debts, if they have to kill me. Yes, for the children, I will!" She paused and looked around slowly, assessing her audience, the way someone preparing to say something untoward would. "You know, I will even lower my flag, if the situation demands it," she said coolly.

"*Eei*, Njunge! What words do you speak now in front of these children here!" protested Nyakiambi even as a round of laughter and sniggers erupted all around. "Can't you weigh your words you shameless woman?"

"And what is wrong with that, Nyakiambi?" countered Njunge, unabashed.

"It is still day, woman, and there are children here, I say. Don't spit such filth, even if you are aggrieved!"

"But isn't it what you women of Kampi Nyasi do?" said Njunge, looking casually around. "Eh? Let's be truthful. And please don't look down. I want you to tell me in honesty- if your child is lying ill in the house staring death in the face and you have no money and you know that someone somewhere has it, won't you do it?"

"You've made your point now, Njunge. Please sit

down," said another elder woman named Njoki, her tone emphatic.

"I was not finished yet, *Cucu*," said Njunge. "Anyway, seeing as you are shy about what you do I will not rub it further in the open wound. As I was saying, my debtors hound me day and night, especially when they know we have received our beggar's pay from the snot-nosed old man in that office down there on Saturdays. But I stand up for my children all the time and tell them they must wait. I must feed the little ones. And there's nowhere anyone can take me. After all I didn't refuse to pay, or did I?"

"You are right, Njunge. What we earn on this farm can hardly take care of our debts," said Wangari, settling down on her *lesso*, which she had spread on the floor. "And maybe it is time we ceased lamenting and *did* something about it."

"*Niguo*. Wangari you are right. We are all almost always indebted to someone," said a stout Akorino woman named Gathoni. "And really we are paid peanuts for our efforts on this farm. Look at all this sack-load I am sitting on for instance, so heavy it breaks your back to lug it all the way up to here. And yet there are three or so I have to gather before the end of the day! And what do I get at the end of it all? A miserly forty shillings- hardly enough to buy a packet of *unga*!"

"You are right. We are only enriching JP and his Njeri while they bleed us dry," seconded another woman at the back of the gathering.

"So, are we going to sit here every other day discussing this and hope it will solve itself?" said Wangari suddenly, springing to her feet. There was a flaming look in her eyes. "Eh? Why is it you keep complaining on and on every other day? Are you sheep that have no brains? Are you children who must sing a nursery rhyme over and over again? Women of Chapa Kazi, I say, we demand a better pay!" she declared, her fist clenched in agitation above her head, bright eyes roving the gathering slowly. "You must stop this fear...this waiting for someone to come along and help. I say you are not cows that are led to the river to drink, prodded along by the herder's stick all the time!"

There was a moment of silence in which the women regarded the stout midget with flaming eyes, stung by her epithet.

And then someone cleared her throat and rose. It was the gangly Njunge.

"But you are one of those people you call cows, Wangari. So how then can you berate us? What have you done for yourself then?"

"I didn't call anyone a cow, Njunge," said Wangari calmly, sweeping around to look at the taller woman. The two were never exactly on friendly terms.

"She meant it only figuratively, Njunge- don't you know Gikuyu?" said Nyakiambi, coming to Wangari's defense.

After a length of time in which the taller woman seemingly digested the answer she sat back at her place on the floor, her long legs stretched in front of her.

Wangari remained standing, her flaming eyes calm.

"I think Wangari is right. We must stop work and demand better pay," said someone softly from the back of the gathering.

A murmur of approval greeted the sentiment.

"There is no other way, women of Chapa Kazi," said Wangari, her tone rising an octave. "*You* must stand up for better pay. No one is going to do it for you."

"Yes. We are not *pundas* to be driven by the stick and given a handful of wilted *sukuma* leaves for our effort!" said a seconder.

All of a sudden there was a measure of excitement in the place, those who had been sleeping on their sacks rising.

"Yes! I say, let's stop this machine today and see where the fat man is going to get his money!"

A few boys trudged up to the shed with their sacks, drawn by the noise of the women. Dumping their loads on the ground, they squatted in the dust at the edge of the gathering, which had grown considerably by then, watching with interest.

A grey-haired woman with a squinted gaze begged to speak with a raised hand and they turned to look at her. Her name was Wamboi, and she was the oldest worker on the farm, having welcomed most of the women on the job.

"You are speaking hot words, women of Kampi Nyasi," said Wamboi in her slow stammer, licking her wet lips as she looked slowly around. The years of bending in the fields had caused damage to her spine so she walked with a permanent stoop. "I have been many years on this farm, and indeed as you say I have hardly grown any richer than the little shack I live in in Kampi Nyasi with my daughter, which is always leaking in the rains. However, I have one worry on my mind," she held up a gnarled index finger that had a disfigured corny nail that was growing back into the root. "However badly you may speak of our employer, which I have no quarrel with, just where else will we get work if we were to be kicked out?"

A moment of silence met the old woman's words, each of the women digesting the concern, which always popped up whenever they got to discuss this matter.

"Look around you, women. There is hardly anyone in the whole of this area with such a big farm as JP's. I am not saying that he is the only employer, but then, even if other jobs were to be found, would all of us be absorbed? Please think carefully and don't act in haste."

As Wamboi reclaimed her place in the dust a young woman with a suckling baby strapped to her breast rose, springing up as if she had been restraining herself on a burning issue all along. "Women, look at this little one here," she said, moving into the clearing at the centre. "Look at his eyes. See?" She pulled back the worn *lesso* covering the child so its snot-spattered face was exposed. "See how white and big the eyes are? See the veins sticking out of his neck and scalp? This child is underfed, and really there is little if any milk left in this wilted breast." She pulled the nipple from the child's mouth and flapped the wasted breast about. "See? It is only cheating him so that he can get to sleep, but really there is nothing! Yes, there is nothing here, I tell you," she said, flapping the breast about, turning around in a circle so that everyone could see.

"Who among you doesn't know that a cow must be fed in order for its udder to swell with milk? Eh?"

A stony silence met her question, the younger suckling women her age in the gathering shuffling their feet uncomfortably. She swung the child back up to the breast and continued, her dark eyes passionate, quite unafraid of addressing the older women.

"We all know that the farmer must toil to provide for the cow in order for it to give something back. The same must apply to us!" She was quite agitated by then, her huge round eyes sticking out, the skin stretching on her bony cheeks.

"Look at me, I have been working years on this farm- they may not be as many as Wamboi's, but still it is quite a while. And yet it is becoming increasingly hard to put a meal on the table at the end of the day for my four children. And where is their father to help me?" she paused rhetorically, glancing around. "The fools are nowhere to lend a hand! I am raising these children all alone, thanks to the *malaya* men of Kampi Nyasi, who plant the seed and disappear into nowhere soon as the child is born. They don't even care a twit where the baby's *uji* will come from. I say, if only for the sake of this child, we must not have fear in our hearts. We must stand up for better pay!"

The men working in the hulling shed stopped their work and stood watching, their greasy hands resting on their hips. The old clerk in the weighing office was disturbed too by the agitation, and he came out and stood watching, the hot midday sun glancing off the thick lenses of his eyeglasses.

"*Turarutithio wira ta digiri...Nituongererwo Mbeca!*" cried Wangari from the middle of the gathering, her voice raised with emotion. "I tell you people, we are worked like donkeys...We must have better pay!" Her plump fist was pumping the air in agitation, her eyes bright with tears.

And all around her the grime-coated women took up the chant, rallying back in unison; "*Nituongererwo Mbeca!*"

Wangari, her excitement mounting, rose to her feet, ready to delve into one of her tirades about those cowards who were good only at dangling their things between their legs and siring what they took utterly no responsibility for. The last speaker had prepared the ground well for the well-known subject among the farmwomen, a turf that Wangari was particularly at her finest strutting. It was largely the reason why she commanded fanatic following among most of the women.

But then, as her moist lips curled up in readiness to plunge into the harangue, eyes aglow with Fenian fervor, she paused.

Coming down the road, straining to lug a sack-load of berries, little Mukami struck a desolate picture.

The load was clearly too much for her, but somehow she hung onto it, trudging one staggery step after another even as it slid lower and lower on her back. She came slowly towards the shed, her teeth dug into her lower lip, as if with determination that she should attain her day's measure, no matter what. Her patched dress hang low at the front, frayed and rent to shreds at the low hem by dew and thorns, barely hanging onto her thin frame.

They all watched as she made one last effort and walked into the shade of the shed, letting go of the sack so it slid to the ground at her feet.

"And this is what you all call a fair day's work, women, is it?" said Wangari softly in the hush that had fallen over the gathering. "All this work this child does, and at the end of it she gets twenty shillings for her troubles? I say, she shouldn't even be working in the fields at all! Same for all these children her age!"

Angry murmurs greeted her words.

As for Mukami, uncertain what it was all about and not comfortable about being the centre of attraction, she moved coyly to the edge of the gathering where she sat down on an old sack and wiped her brow on her sleeve, letting out her breath slowly.

In the ensuing confused murmuring one of the

women by name Waithera, a usually reserved worker who spoke only to her close confidants rose slowly, lifting her sack onto her back. They watched her walk towards the factory entrance, uncertain what her intention was.

At the factory gate Waithera lowered her sack and, holding it firmly by the base, emptied the ripe berries in the middle of the road.

"What has got into Waithera?" asked someone, confused. "What is she doing?"

There was a lull in which the question hang, unanswered. What followed was rather spontaneous, sudden and unexplained. Like a single insect bite that suddenly whips up a stampede in a calm herd. All of a sudden the once peaceful gathering stirred, the grimy farmhands rising. The women, like a pack of agitated hounds on a spoor, scrambled for their sacks and hurried towards the gate. They were all yelling at the top of their voices, "*Turarutithio wira ta digiri... Nituongererwo Mbeca!*"

***

The farm guards were gathered outside the little hut by the farm entrance spectating a game of *ajua* between Sempei and a crafty contender called Moloyi. It was a tense duel because they were playing for money. It was as Sempei was preparing to gather the pebbles in the hollow on his side of the long wooden board that they heard the noises from the direction of the river.

Puzzled, they abandoned the game and rose, reaching for their clubs.

"That sounds like *kisirani* brewing to me," said one of the youthful guards, his face darkening. He was adjusting the strap of his curved *akala* sandal that had been fashioned out of an old motorbike tyre.

"You are right. It is those women of Kampi Nyasi- I know their voices."

The eldest among them, a grey-haired tall man with stooping shoulders rose and stepped aside from the group, spitting tobacco residue in the grass, ear cocked.

"Yes, you are right," he said, nodding. "Go up and look, Sempei!"

Gathering the folds of his bright red *shuka* Sempei ran up to the watchtower and climbed up the creaky wooden ladder two rungs at a time, the binoculars he had grabbed from the hut dangling around his neck.

He panned slowly from the bridge all the way to the factory, taking in the riotous scene that bobbed in and out of focus as he fiddled with the knob that adjusted the lenses. And as the riot registered, he dropped the field glasses and climbed down the ladder, shouting orders to the regiment of red *shukas* that had assembled at the foot of the tower, brandishing bows, arrows and short knobkerries that had heavy iron nuts attached to the clubbing end. Sheathed in the folds of their *shukas* were their sharpened bush *simis*.

Fright was clearly written on Sempei's face even as he dispatched the guards.

On second thought he ran to the farmhouse to place a call to JP from the hallway phone, seeing as Madam was not around to make a decision. There was the fear that the crowd could get out of hand, in which case they would need reinforcement.

"What did you say, Sempei...a riot?" barked JP at the other end when the connection finally went through.

"Yes, *Mzee*. The women have gone on strike. It must be that *kisirani* woman Wangari at it again."

"Well, deal with her, then...deal with all of them! Isn't that what I pay you to do?"

"They have gone wild, *Mzee*, ...they are pouring all the coffee in the road."

"What...?" There was a prolonged silence at the other end, in which the farm-owner's breath came clearly in angry gasps.

"Sempei! ...*Get the gates wide open*," he said in a dangerous whisper. "The Police will be there in a while!"

"Yes, *Mzee*," said the tense guard, even as the line went dead.

When the navy police truck swung through the farm gates a while later the riot had gone completely out of hand. The factory was crawling with angry workers who were venting their anger on the machines. A man carrying a huge tree limb moved between the rows of drying racks hitting the trays and scattering the hardening white berries all over, shouting at the top of his voice. The old man who usually manned the racks watched him from atop the hill, leaning on his white cane, fright in his grey eyes because he had had to run as fast as his bony legs would bear him to get away from the mob.

A band of women had taken over the huge brick-walled store, chasing away the loaders. They now moved from row to row thrusting machetes and other sharp objects into the sacks. They applauded gleefully every time a hole was opened in the sack and the dried berries poured onto the floor.

Some other women had emptied the sluice gate and flooded the hulling pit with water. In this they poured some of the *mbuni* berries that they could carry over, applauding as they twirled and twirled in the foul-smelling frothy water and went on down the grime-coated channel towards the river.

A group of the younger women, in the grip of the excitement, dragged up the old pallet truck used in the store and loaded it with sacks and other movable equipment they could find in the machine shed. In a collective *harambee* effort they pushed it up to the edge of the murram-covered yard and gave one collective yell, heaving and sending it over the raised cement kerb. A wild cheer filled the place as the heavy pallet tumbled down the hill towards the river, wobbling left and right as it gained momentum on the steep incline.

One of the old farm tractors was coming up to the factory from the side JP was cultivating for a new planting when a band of young men suddenly pounced on it from the pathside bushes, climbing over the sides of the empty trailer. The startled driver didn't have time enough to run, and there was little else he could do but cooperate with the excited commandeers, who were waving twigs and tree branches in his face, singing hoarsely at the top of their voices.

When they got to the factory yard one of the young men pulled out the jerrican stuck behind the driver's seat, which was usually used to fetch fuel when the old tractor stalled out in the fields. Rummaging among the broken wrenches and other accessories stored in the narrow space he yanked out a plastic hose, which he inserted into the fuel tank. He then proceeded to siphon the contents into the jerrican.

The overwhelmed driver watched aghast, wondering what the youths were up to. It was frightening to think what one of those cigarette butts the youths were passing around so liberally could do if it got close enough.

And all over in this frenzied confusion the excited workers chanted the by then infectious call, "*Turarutithio wira ta digiri...Nituongererwo Mbeca!*" waving twigs and their shirts above their heads. Their voices rang out across the valley, echoing off the facing hillside.

The Maasai guards arrived just in time to stop the youths dousing the clerk's office with the fuel. They launched at them, clubbing haphazardly left and right.

And as the yelping youths scattered, some of them regrouped and charged at the guards, brandishing timber bars and tree limbs.

On the fringes of the fierce fight that ensued the women formed into a circle, similarly armed with sticks and tree saplings.

"Castrate the bastards!" yelled a stout little woman called Wanjiru, her shrill voice high-pitched with excitement. "Go for the mad dogs...Go, sons of our strong loins!" she yelled, launching at one of the guards with a piece of thick rubber hose that she had found in the tool shed.

For a while the Maasai guards appeared to hold their fort, lashing viciously at the farmhands with their hippo-hide and rubber *nyaunyo* whips. But then the pressure mounted even as the farmhands cried out in pain, the wounded charging back with rocks and other missiles, baying for blood. Meanwhile those who were not in the thick of it called for reinforcement, screaming at the top of their voices. Soon it became such that the guards were hemmed in by angry workers on all sides.

There was only one way for the Maasai guards to go as the crowds of yelling workers built; and it was to find an opening in the stampede and run for their lives.

This was the scene that greeted the police truck as it sped downhill towards the river, siren blaring.

A few Maasai guards had hurriedly clambered over the sides of the truck, emboldened at the reinforcement after their failed earlier attempt to disperse the mob.

As the truck hurtled downhill, the striking workers stopped the destruction they were engaged in and stood watching it crest the rise in the road and swing at top speed towards the dip of the bridge. A pall of conspiratorial silence settled over the bands of workers as they watched the truck, a fiery boldness glinting in the depths of their eyes. In different circumstances there would have been fright at the sight of the police in full riot gear.

The driver, in the full clutch of the mounting adrenalin, swung the truck over the brow and froze on seeing the stretch of red spread out on the road ahead of him. On instinct he stepped on the brakes, causing the wheels to lock with a protesting screech that could be heard a mile away. The officers seated beside him in the cab, unprepared for the sudden braking, were hurled face-first into the dashboard as the squelchy slide on flattened red berries started underneath the truck. The huge truck, propelled by the weight of the officers in the back, slid downhill like a runaway farm cart, skidding from side to side as the driver frantically pumped the brakes and wrung on the wheel.

On ahead the bridge drew closer and closer, even as the truck gained momentum. Some of the officers, realizing what was happening, vaulted over the side of the truck and jumped, rolling into the grass where they lay clutching their broken limbs, moaning pitifully. The driver, on seeing the futility of his effort on the mucoury carpet of red, abandoned his duty and opened his door, flinging himself into the hurtling bushes.

As curled-up human cannon balls continued launching themselves off the sides of the wobbly truck it slid lower and lower until it was onto the narrow bridge. The driverless truck, like a blinded giant, remained frozen a while at the rail-less edge, as if contemplating the suicide dive. Then it bucked and slowly tipped over, shooting nose-first into the swirling brown river underneath, egged on by the frantic struggles and yells of the frightened officers still trapped in the back.

***

It was the workers who eventually came to the rescue. After watching for a while from a distance, frozen in shock at the crash, it was Wangari who first stepped out from behind a clump of bush where she had taken refuge from the beatings of the fiery guards. She moved up into the clearing and turned to the other workers, her shredded clothing trailing behind her like old sacking caught on a farmyard barbed fence. Waving her beefy arms above her head she signaled them to come out.

They approached the scene, wary at first because they were uncertain how the police would react. But seeing that the few officers out of the water were helpless the workers hurriedly formed a column at the side of the bridge, beckoning to each other to get closer. Some of the officers trapped in the wreckage in the swirling brown river waved at the farmhands, urging them to jump in and help them, fear in their erstwhile stony eyes.

The truck was half submerged in the deep brown river, the cab buried deep into the soft mud. A young man by name Chege pulled off his shirt and, rolling up the leggings of his worn trousers, squatted at the edge of the river and dived inside. He slipped under to help an officer who was trapped in the cab break open the windshield. He reemerged shortly, brushing muddy water from his face, and called for someone on the bank to throw him a rock.

After a little struggle underwater with the rock he came up, dragging the officer commanding the troupe by the scruff of his neck.

Two more young men dived in and they helped him haul the hefty officer out through the hole created in the window.

The women waiting on the bank held out their hands to receive the fat officer, helping carry him to a grassy spot where they lay him down on the grass and set to work getting him to bring up the water he had swallowed. They unbuckled his belt and one of them leaned on his fat belly, pressing with the flat of her hands.

For a while she applied and eased the pressure, everyone watching the dark officer's face anxiously. And then the huge officer gurgled and a line of muddy slime slid down his chin. After a couple more attempts they were able to get him to stir out of his daze, opening his red-rimmed eyes and staring uncertainly about, just before his huge frame was seized by a bout of coughing.

Across on the other bank a human chain was passing the injured officers from one callused set of hands to another, loading them into the trailer of the old tractor that had driven up. As they worked, the farmhands tried all they could to comfort the writhing and moaning officers.

When JP arrived half an hour later, a police ambulance in tow, he found that the farmhands had already dispatched the first trailer-load of the injured to hospital. There was a look of barely disguised loathing on his face as he climbed out of his car and walked up to the roadside. Wangari, her brow moist with the effort, paused from her task of setting a broken leg in a crude splinter fashioned out of coffee branches and looked up, a motherly look in her round dark eyes. "We did the best we could, *Mzee*," she said softly, sighing.

"So I see," said JP acidly, his flaming eyes roving the scene, assessing the damage.

For a while he looked towards the submerged truck in the muddy river, and the muddied young men hacking away at it with axes to free more casualties. He took in the human chain that passed on the injured up to the tractors.

And then, turning to a senior officer close by he summoned him with a flick of his finger. They moved a little distance away from the makeshift first-aid point and conversed a while. Shortly after JP stepped away and climbed into the car, ordering the driver to drive to the factory.

***

The Police came for Wangari two days later.

It was a Sunday afternoon and the women were sitting in the shade of their doorways after the midday meal. Some were still in their church clothes, the spotless white dresses that had come out of the clothes trunk awaiting their wash later in the day and a coal iron before returning to the mothballed depths.

Further down the street the service at the church at the end of the block was still dragging on. The drumming was a monotonous *du-dum...dum!, du-dum...dum!*, stopping and then starting again, the beat lagging, as if the drummer was ready to break for lunch. In the intermittent lapses in the drumming the pastor's voice rose to a wavery crescendo, admonishing the sinful and exorcising demons in the repentants, the

thunderous spats punctuated by calls of halleluiah...
halleluiah! ... from the faithful.

In the shade of the roof eave outside the pregnant
nanny goat lay chewing cud, leaning against the rotting
wall, its splayed front hooves spread. In the fine dust
besides the children played, occasionally stopping to
retrieve the ball from the murky open drain running
the length of the street, soiling their Sunday best in the
process. They were oblivious of the pastor's charged
remonstrations.

Wangari was talking to the woman who lived across
from her in the facing block as she winnowed the grain
that would go into that evening's meal of *githeri*. Her
daughter Ciiru was inside washing the lunch dishes.
The other woman paused from plaiting her hair and
looked towards the river.

"What is it?" said Wangari, following her gaze.

"Look."

Through the gap at the end of the two long grass-
thatched blocks a section of the earth road was visible,
winding downhill through the coffee estate towards the
factory.

A navy blue van was coming down the road, raising
a column of dust in its wake.

They watched the van come slowly towards Kampi
Nyasi. It drew to a stop at the block next to Wangari's
and two police officers jumped out. Glancing casually
around they walked towards the group of villagers who
had gathered in the street, mostly curious children
and a few women.

"We are here to see Wangari," announced the one
in a khaki uniform, swinging his swagger stick at the
hip casually. "Does any one of you know where her
house is?"

A stout dark woman stepped forward, sweeping

185

her naked pot-bellied child behind her.

"What do you want with Wangari?" she demanded, suspicion in her eyes.

"We need her to answer a few questions at the station. She will be back shortly," said the smiling officer.

There was silence, in which the villagers looked uncertainly at each other. The police officers waited, glancing casually around, the looks on their faces carefully controlled, civil.

"What station are you from?" said someone at the back of the growing gathering.

The officer in the khaki uniform answered, still smiling casually at the crowd.

"I don't believe them," said another in a whisper, hand cupped over her friend's ear.

"Yes, I don't trust these people an inch," whispered the other.

"Why should we believe you?" the villager who had spoken first said aloud, tightening the knot in her *lesso* cloth as if she intended to take on the officer.

"We don't mean any trouble, women," said the officer, still fiddling with his stick, his manner deceptively civil, even coy. "Don't you think we appreciate what you did for our officers the other day? It is just a little formality that must go into the book, and then she'll be back."

There was an uncomfortable silence in which the villagers consulted in muted tones.

Wangari, who was standing at the back of the gathering, saved them the trouble by stepping through into the clearing. Her daughter Ciiru was hanging onto her skirt, fearful for her mother. As for Wangari, she was visibly calm and composed.

The officer stepped forward, his hand outstretched,

the cunning smile playing on his lips. He seemed to recognize her.

"*Jambo*, Mama!" he said, taking her hand in a firm handshake. "We heard about what you did for our colleagues, and we are very impressed. The OCPD would like a word with you. He would like to thank you personally for your effort. That is why we are here today. Now, will you kindly come with us to the station?"

Wangari sized up the officer, trying to discern a grain of cunning in his manner. Then she looked back at the anxious villagers gathered around them.

Someone in the crowd said in a loud whisper, "I don't believe this man. Why didn't the '*osi*' come himself if at all he needed to thank us?"

"Don't go," said another. "He appears a little too slick to me, this tall one."

"Yes. They are playing a game," acquiesced another, coughing uncomfortably.

The village children had by then abandoned their play, gathering around the blue van, inching even closer so they could touch it and have a peek inside the cabin. The officer at the wheel was smiling stiff-lipped at them, as if he meant to shoo them away, but was restraining himself.

Wangari shrugged and, taking a deep breath patted her daughter on the head and walked gracefully towards the parked Land Rover, adjusting the scarf on her head. "I think I will go see what this '*osi*' wants with me," she said aloud, squaring her rounded shoulders. "I am not at war with him after all, am I?"

The officer in khaki uniform smiled brightly at her gesture and showed her into the cab, holding the door open for her. Nodding his thanks for her cooperation, he climbed in after her and pulled the door shut. The van started up soon after, turning slowly in the street and driving off in the direction of the river, even as it occurred rather late to the villagers that someone should have accompanied her.

That was the last the people of Kampi Nyasi saw of Wangari.

***

Two other women, Waitherera and the Akorino Gathoni were picked up at the tool shed as they prepared to collect their work tools in the morning.

JP had been standing outside the toolshed as usual, muddy from inspecting the cattle yard.

Waitherera came up in the company of another woman trading the day's gossip and entered the shed.

As she left with her sack draped on her shoulder she felt a tap on her shoulder.

Turning, one of the tall Maasai guards jerked a finger in her face, indicating the jeep parked close by. Before she knew what was happening she was being propelled by the elbow and bundled into the car. Inside the two cops in civilian who had been waiting for her smiled humourlessly at her, motioning to her to sit still with their rubber truncheons.

Gathoni was picked up in a similar manner shortly thereafter.

The jeep sped off soon after with the two women sandwiched between the beefy officers.

As the vehicle turned out of the farm gates the guards hurriedly ringed around the scene, scaring off the workers who had started gathering as the news of the arrest spread.

This time around the guards had reinforcement. A pick-up truckload of armed police spent the entire day patrolling the farm, their anti-riot tin helmets pulled low over their stony red eyes that darted this way and that, butting anyone they perceived to be idling along with a swing of their metal-toed boots.

Chapter Nineteen

THE shrill ringing of the alarm bedside clock shattered the peace of the lawyer's dream about a silent place where the stream steals its way through whispering trees and overgrown rocks. She jumped awake with a start, banging the old wind-action Jock clock that was the surest relic of life with father. The mystery about why it had waken her while the rays of the sun were yet to filter through the parting in the heavy brocade blinds was soon explained by the realization that she had set it to ring earlier than usual as she retired to bed the day before.

"Damn!" she pushed away the old goose-down eiderdown quilt that had covered her folks since she couldn't remember when and swung her legs out of the wide old-fashioned carved oak bed with its lumpy mattress.

Wrapping her mother's nightgown closer about her she slipped her feet in the fur slippers and padded her way to the kitchen, the familiar creak of the old floorboards accompanying her like an old dog.

She took out two eggs from the old kerosene-powered refrigerator that hummed like a harassed tractor and broke them into a chipped enamel bowl. Then she took a couple of sausages and a partly-eaten chicken leg and put them in the microwave- the only modern equipment that had as yet found its way into the kitchen- and set the timer.

Turning on the wooden Sanyo radio so the old *Kumepambazuka* Congolese rhumbas wafted through the corridor she padded out into the bathroom to have her bath.

The two days that she had skipped this familiar routine confined to bed by the persistent headache that had been coming on and off for the past month made going through the motions feel like the ringing of the bells that first day at school after a long holiday break.

But of one thing she was grateful even as she set out early to resume work; the headache was gone.

Exactly an hour and a half later she was seated in her seven-year-old Toyota Corolla, which was fairly unnoticeable amongst the flashy SUVs that her neighbours along Kiambu Road drove to work, waiting for the crawling traffic to ease on.

She was trying not to glance at the morning paper because she knew it was a bad habit while driving. She had decided to go via Wangige along the Kikuyu route on to town because she needed to pass by a client who worked in Kikuyu town. Her eyes were glued to the misty window on her side, half conscious of the whorls of mist that had started rolling in from the Limuru direction as the cold season started to set in. As her mind wandered through the numerous cases that she had had to put off due to the headache she became vaguely conscious of something by the roadside that was intruding in her thoughts.

The donkey that was harnessed to the cart was old and bony, its ribs sticking out through the leathery skin. A large festering sore covered its flank, attracting a swarm of blue flies even this early in the morning. It stood by the roadside, large ears moving slowly back and forth, waiting for the car that had blocked its way to move on into the line of traffic.

The little cart was laden with freshly cut nappier grass, and sitting atop it was a shabbily dressed young man...or was it a boy? It was difficult to tell because the frayed old cloth cap he wore slouched at an angle over his face.

However, it was not that, nor the donkey's condition that attracted the lawyer's attention.

The boy was engaged in some play with a huge glove he wore over his right hand that was shaped like a mitt- or a wicket-keeper's glove- and which was made of some thick tough plastic material. He was taking off the glove and putting it back on, and in that brief moment that it was off, the lawyer thought she missed to see the hand it was supposed to cover. Otherwise her eyes were playing tricks with her.

With the curiosity that can only be aroused in a lawyer of long practice she wrung on the wheel and pulled over sharply onto the shoulder.

The boy, who was in the process of removing the glove, pushed it hurriedly back in place. He picked up the rubber *nyaunyo* whip atop the mound of fodder and prepared to lash the donkey.

"Jambo!" said Miss Nyokabi in as pleasant a way as her years of practice had coached her.

But the boy had already lashed at the donkey and it was moving forward. Miss Nyokabi ran alongside the cart and persisted, made even the more curious by the boy's strange reaction, determined to climb onto the cart if need be.

Seeing that the lady was reaching for his hand the boy slithered off the cart and hopped onto the ground, breaking into a run.

But then Miss Nyokabi had not been the athletics champion at Kenya High for nothing. Kicking off her pointed office shoes, she hitched up her skirt and gave chase.

Curious motorists stared after them, wondering

what the smartly dressed lady could be chasing the urchin for. Perhaps he had stolen her purse...?

By the time the lawyer grabbed the boy's coat and swung him around, she was out of breath. It had been a long chase.

"*Ehe*? Why are you running, *kijana*?" she said, looking at the gloved hand. "Something the matter with your hand there?"

Now that he had lost the chase the boy stood nervously by, quite fidgety and ill at ease.

He looked left and right, searching for an opportunity to escape.

But obviously the lawyer wasn't going to allow that. She covered him well, like a hunting dog might a cornered rabbit.

"What is your name?"

The boy glanced nervously left and right, and then at the lawyer. There was fright in his eyes, and his wiry body kept jerking, as if he was testing the firmness of the lawyer's grip. "Come on, you won't escape me that easily," said the lawyer, applying pressure to the wrist. "You had better tell me your name, and then I'll let you go."

"Ndonga," piped the boy.

"Good. Is that your donkey?"

"Uh-uhm!" he hesitated a while, his eyes darting. The lawyer nodded for him to carry on. "It belongs to JP. I was only sent to fetch fodder. I...I d-didn't steal it, Madam," he added, begging to be believed.

There was something vaguely familiar about the boy now that they were standing close enough, although the lawyer couldn't tell what. "You didn't go to school today?" she said, peering into his shifty eyes.

For answer the boy averted his gaze and shook

192

his head. The lawyer thought she saw a wistful look cross his face, but shortly the impertinence returned.

"Why?"

A mute silence met the question.

"So, why were you running away?" said the lawyer, changing tact. "I am certain you had done nothing wrong. Here, let me see your hand."

The boy tensed all of a sudden, giving a frantic struggle. But the lawyer was prepared for it, and she grabbed his wrist in her vice-like grip. With the other hand she loosened the strange glove that was strapped in place with frayed Velcro strips.

A faint odour rose from the open glove, like that which a fish three days out of the water might give off.

"No," cried the boy fearfully, tears glistening in his eyes. "Don't!" He grabbed at the lawyer's hand and tried to shake her off.

With a mounting sense of mystery the lawyer went on to pull it right off.

"What...?" she said. But the question died on her lips as she gaped in shock at the mangled stump of hard bone and twisted tissue that was hidden behind the glove.

"JP said never to take it off...especially around strangers," mumbled the boy, his words punctuated by pitiful sobs.

"My God, what happened to you?" she turned the wasted wrist around and examined the underside.

"I was injured as a boy...I don't remember," said the boy, still struggling to free himself, albeit feebly now that the secret of his hand had been exposed.

"Look, please don't lie to me," said the lawyer, looking him straight in the eye. "I know it was some accident, and I need to know."

"Please let me go, Madam," moaned the boy, the tears now flowing freely down his face. "I will be late, and JP will give me a thrashing. *Please.*"

"I will let you go in a short while, I promise," said the lawyer, her tone persuasive. "I only need to know what happened to your hand, that's all." She got down on one knee and held the boy's wrist, angling her face, which had softened, a motherly look in her eyes. "I am your friend, and I don't intend to harm you. Come on, you can trust me."

He looked into her eyes, figuring. Then his tear-washed gaze shifted to his donkey, which, left on its own, was grazing the lush roadside grass as it awaited its minder.

"Come on Ndonga," she whispered. "Tell me, what happened? And who is this JP?"

She was still trying to place the boy, convinced that he was not a stranger. But somehow she couldn't seem to remember where she had seen him.

For a while there it appeared like the boy was going to open up. But then he reconsidered, the nervousness returning to his face. "No, I can't tell you, Madam. I am sorry. But I will be in great trouble. No." He shook his head, looking towards his grazing donkey.

The resolve had weakened slightly, and the lawyer knew that he was afraid to look at her because she was starting to succeed in winning his trust. She had trained herself to read people's thoughts on her job.

"Look, Ndonga, I am sorry too," she said softly, slackening her hold on his wrist, but still not letting go. "But then, if you so insist, then we'll just have to wait here until you do. There is no other way."

There was a moment of silence in which the boy arranged and rearranged his thoughts, contemplating.

"And I don't think you are a stranger to me at all. I must have seen you somewhere before. It is where that I can't seem to remember. Perhaps you'll remind me?"

After a length of time in which neither budged the boy turned back to face her, blinking his eyes rapidly to stem the tears. Wiping the running snot on his sleeve, he sniffed and said, "You must first promise not to tell anyone, Madam."

"Here, use my handkerchief here," said the lawyer, handing her her pressed hanky. "You have my word. I won't tell a soul. And you can call me simply Julia. Remember I don't mean to harm you. I am your friend."

"You see you will get not just myself in lots of trouble, but my mother and sister as well; and even Juma- I think."

"You have my word, Ndonga."

"Alright," said the boy, drying his eyes with the handkerchief.

***

Half an hour later the lawyer walked the boy back to where his donkey was grazing, her plans for the day gone into disarray all of a sudden. With the promise to come and see them and a pat on his head, she helped him climb up onto the cart and stood by as he lashed the donkey and started off.

Only after the cart had turned into the narrow overgrown track that issued off the road did she walk back to where she had left her shoes and climb back into the car. And as she started the motor and signaled to get into the road, that day she had gone to the mission hospital in Kikuyu came back clearly in her mind, same to the gruff overweight man who had refused to talk to her. It was a strange coincidence indeed.

Chapter Twenty

MRS. Nyokabi sat in the Kenchic Café on Moi Avenue watching the Nairobians waddle past the shop window as they got home from another busy Friday. In the street the old Kenya Buses jostled for right of way with shuttle vans and cabs, brakes squealing as the horns blared out the drivers' rage. In between the throngs of city dwellers wove, staring up indifferently at the cursing driver who had been forced to stand on the brakes to let them pass. On the sidewalk the drone of the hawkers pinged like a faulty siren from one end of the street to the other, their multi-faceted wares spread right into the way so the passersby had little choice but to snake along the narrow leeway allowed them and buy something.

The light in the café window came on as dusk settled, lighting up the fried chicken turning slowly on the barbeque machine. Above the frying chicken the café's neon sign that had one letter missing started blinking. All over the dust-crusted streetlights slowly blinked on, throwing a spot of amber around the lamppost.

Further up on the first floor the disco thumped like a wet drum as the dee-jay cranked up the volume for the 'party hour'; the object of the little gathering of skimpily-dressed teenagers in the taxi rank waiting for the bouncers at the door to screen them.

Mrs. Nyokabi twirled her coffee slowly and drank, watching the city with a little disinterest. She had bought a bag of fries which she had generously drowned in tomato sauce and some other bottled brown stuff on the table that didn't have a name like everyone in the place seemed to be doing. Her half chicken was long gone, but the fries remained mostly untouched. She wasn't really hungry.

A lame street vendor was engaged in a heated argument with a fat heavily-made-up woman who had tipped over his tray of sweets and other confectioneries as she passed, the vendor gesturing angrily with one of his crutches into the woman's face. A little distance away a street urchin who had been lolling by the kerb with his head resting on an oily sack, sniffing at a bottle half-full of Con-Ta adhesive rose and moved slowly behind the line of parked cars. Two of his friends peeked round the hedge of shaggy bougainvillea lining the street and signaled. Their faces were darkened with tar from warming themselves around a bonfire lit from an old car tire, eyes glazed from sniffing the adhesive the whole day.

The boy with a sack ducked behind one of the saloon cars, reaching into the pocket of his grubby jeans for a small screwdriver. He emerged shortly, cradling a windshield wiper and a car front lamp that had its ripped wires dangling. He joined his friends and they slinked away casually into the jostling crowds in the street.

A little distance away a little girl walked up to a shabbily dressed woman squatting on the kerb and bared her palm. The woman snatched away the few coins in the girl's hand and berated her sharply for a job poorly done, gesturing angrily with her hands, before sending her off with a sharp pinch on the cheek. The crying girl collected her dog-eared exercise book on the dusty pavement together with the stub of a pencil and rejoined the thronging crowds on the street, pushing her book in the way of a respectable-looking fare she had carefully espied and begging that he 'sponsors' her. Behind her the dour-faced woman put the coins in her bosom and swaddled herself in her dirty *shuka*, going back to her glue sniffing as she watched the little girls.

Ms Nyokabi watched the woman for a while, her mind racing.

On impulse she rose and cashed her bill and walked out of the shop, leaving the bag of fries on the table.

The street woman was evidently wary as the well-dressed lady approached and stopped. She quickly reached into the folds of her *shuka* for a hidden weapon, probably a bottle with a broken-off base, her wiry frame poised to run.

"*Habari*!" said the lawyer, squatting beside her, smiling brightly. "How would you like to be bought a new dress, Mama?"

The street woman, puzzled by the question, stared back stonily at her, her face hostile, and the lawyer had to repeat the offer.

"*Wee Mathee wacha vacko! Kwani umetumwa kwangu?*" said the woman in a drooling tongue, gathering her skirts in readiness to rise. "*Umeona kaa sina nguo? Wee ishia!*" she spat out defiantly, waving a grease-crusted finger, the hostile look on her face acquiring a dangerous shade.

"*Hapana, Mama*, please listen to me," said the lawyer persuasively. "I am serious. I want to buy you a new dress. Over there," she gestured towards the brightly-lit exhibition shops across the street. "It is true."

It took a lot of persuasion to get the woman to walk into the shop. And even more to get the attendants to fit her for a new georgette dress and a cashmere sweater that had tags on them that could only be conceived in the street woman's wildest dreams curled up on a rain-washed pavement. Only when the lawyer took out her purse and showed her some colour did the cynicism on the face of the salesgirl turn to warmth.

When she emerged from behind the little screen at the back of the shop the street woman was even the more surprised when the lady with a fat purse took her smelly bundle of old clothes and put them into a crisp paper bag, which she clutched under her arm. Leaving both the salesgirl and the street woman staring after her Ms Nyokabi strode out into the street and walked up to her car parked outside the fast-food shop.

***

When the workers reported for work at Chapa Kazi the following morning they found JP already up, leaning against the cattle shed watching as they trooped to the store and out. Flanking him were four lanky guards clad in their habitual red *shukas* that revealed the *simis*, clubs and other weapons tucked into their ammo belts. A handful more were loitering in the vicinity, eyeing the workers with hard stares.

A little woman clad in a tattered old dress that reached down to her worn canvas shoes detached herself from the bushy hedge lining the road a little distance from the farm gate and fell in behind a line of women headed for the *panya* entrance. She was hugging the dirty *shuka* close about her, her nylon headscarf tied such that it passed low just above her eyes.

As they crept into the opening in the hedge the woman at the rear of the file stopped to glance at the little woman, a little puzzled because she had never seen her face at the farm.

"*Ni kwega,*" she called in greeting.

"*Ee, ni kwega,*" mumbled the shuka-clad woman.

The other woman shrugged and walked on into the narrow entrance. She was probably a new comer from one of the neighbouring farms, she thought as she resumed trading the morning talk with the other women.

Juma too was puzzled as he handed her a sack and a rusty tin from the pile in the store, trying to remember when he had last seen her on the farm, and where.

With her sack tucked firmly underneath her arm and the old tin clutched in her frozen hands she followed the other women out of the yard. She barely raised her gaze shortly later when two of the guards at the other end seized a young man the farm-owner had fingered in the queue and dragged him away between them towards the back of the chicken house.

As they followed the path into the maize field headed for the coffee estate the agonized cry of the young man who had been led away suddenly rent the air, sharp and piercing, like a pig's. The farmhands shivered, a pall of silence descending over them as they quickened their step towards their workstations.

Chapter Twenty One

THE wheelbarrow hit a rut in the dusty path and teetered on the brink of tipping over. Ndonga stuck out his foot and fought it, wrenching the slipping lumped load of fresh nappier that he had strapped down with sisal rope back into balance. Locking the sweat-slicked handle bar of the barrow firmly in the crook of his bad hand he heaved with all his might, the puny calf muscles on his thin legs taut, veins sticking out on his temples. The heavy barrow rolled on, wobbly wheel creaking from lack of greasing, and crunched to a stop in the shade of an avocado tree growing by the pathside.

He flopped down at the foot of the tree and rested his tortured back against the rough trunk, his breath escaping him in a gush. In the stifling midday heat his nylon shirt was drenched in sweat, sticking to his back and sides. He removed the shirt and fanned himself, watching the droplets of sweat on his sternum roll down his belly. He was very thirsty.

He had started dozing against the trunk of the tree, lulled by the cool breeze blowing through the swaying maize plants when he jumped with a start, conscious of a presence. The first thought that came to his mind was one of the mean guards who had chanced upon him as he slept.

"It is a tough job feeding the cattle, isn't it, *kijana yangu*?" said the *shuka*-clad woman who appeared down the bend in the path, smiling. "It is just you I was looking for."

Ndonga started, staring up at the woman, not amused by the creeping way she had stole up to him.

"Remember me?" she said with a smile, taking off the dirty *shuka* that covered her head, partly hiding her face.

"Aah! It is you!" Only when he looked closer did he recognize the face of the woman who had chased him the previous week on his way from collecting nappier.

"Aha! It is me alright." She squatted down beneath the tree, gathering the old dress in her lap.

"What are you doing here, Miss?" said Ndonga, clearly surprised. "How did you get here?"

"I told you I would be back, didn't I?" said the woman, smiling. "Well, here I am. Now sit down and let's talk. I don't think I have much time."

"But...does JP know you are here?" Ndonga's voice dropped to a whisper as the surprise on his face changed to fear.

"Certainly not. And I don't think he would be very amused if he did."

"I see. So you *stole* your way in, didn't you?"

"As you can see." She indicated her ragged clothing, her arms spread out. "It obviously involved a bit of cunning."

"*Phew!*" said Ndonga, squatting beside her. "You really are very brave. You followed the path I told you?"

"I have a very good memory, Ndonga."

"I hope the guards don't catch you. You know they beat up one of the boys by name Githinji real bad just this morning. He was caught stealing cabbages at the other end."

"Really? I heard someone cry out when we were leaving the store this morning," said the lawyer, her eyebrows raised.

"They beat him up real bad. He was carried to Kampi Nyasi on his mother's back. He couldn't even walk."

"That is a horrible thing to do to someone- just for stealing cabbages!"

"Indeed. That's why I am afraid for you. The guards have got real mean, especially after the riot on the farm. You heard the Police took away Wangari from Kampi Nyasi on Sunday? And she was not alone. They seized some other women along with her. They say they were taken to the cells."

"Is it?" said the lawyer, surprised at the news. "Who else was arrested?"

"Just the three of them. But the Police have been coming on the farm. They say they are looking for the boys who burned down one of JP's tractors. Of course they haven't caught anyone. They all disappeared from the village Sunday night and have not been seen on the farm since. All the same it is very scary. Hardly anyone talks about the strike or Wangari and her friends."

"Tch! Tch! Tch! That is a bad thing," said the lawyer, shaking her head, her brow creased.

"You are sure someone won't find you here?" said the boy frightfully, glancing down the winding path just in case. "You know the guards sometimes come by this way."

"I hope they don't. I must do what I have to while I am here. Now, where is your mother? I need to speak to her. I need to speak to Juma as well. I saw him on the farm, and I suspect he smelt something fishy about me when our eyes met. Do you think you can get them to see me?"

"I already told Mother about you and your plan to help us. She was rather scared at the suggestion.

She wasn't sure it would work. She is in the kitchen preparing porridge. I can sneak into the yard and pass your message to her. I am sure no one will see me."

"Please do," said the lawyer. "It is important that I speak to her, and possibly the boy who was beaten this morning as well. I need to get some details from them. Now, be a good boy and hurry along. And remember; don't whisper a word to anybody else about this, will you?"

"Alright," said the boy nodding. "Wait here for me. I will be back shortly. You must hide deep in the maize just incase JP or one of the guards chances to come this way."

"That I will, my boy."

Ndonga rose and put on his shirt, readying the glove on his hand for the task of pushing the wheelbarrow. And as he staggered off, swaying along with the laden barrow, the lawyer hid back inside the knit maize to wait, impressed by the boy's skill and strength.

He appeared a while later, his mother in tow. There was a wary look on the woman's face, and she kept looking about nervously, as if she expected someone to appear down the path any time.

"*Habari, Mama*," said the lawyer, emerging from the knit maize plants, her hand extended. "I am glad you agreed to come."

"You are the *wakili*?" said the woman, plainly surprised.

"I am indeed," said Miss Nyokabi with a bright smile. "My name is Nyokabi. And don't let these shabby clothes fool you. I practice law alright."

"Well, you hardly look like a *wakili*."

"There was no other way to get in here, you see."

They shook hands and moved into the cover of the hanging branch of the avocado tree.

"My name is Njambi. My boy told me about you," said the farmwoman nervously, wiping at her moist brow with the edge of her *lesso* cloth.

"And you know what? Ndonga, surprisingly, is no stranger to me! I have been thinking, and now I know where I first met your son. It when he was brought to the hospital in Kikuyu after his hand was injured."

"Is it?" said the farmwoman, surprised.

"Indeed I must say I was a bit curious about the boy's injury at the time, regardless of my own illness that had taken me there. But then I didn't really give it much thought after. That is until I saw him one day driving his donkey along the road. I suppose he told you about the incident?"

"Indeed. He said you can run pretty fast for a woman your age."

The lawyer smiled, a little embarrassed at the compliment. "It is good to meet you, *wakili*. Still," she scratched at her head thoughtfully, "as much as I appreciate your concern, really am scared about this. I cannot pretend."

"I understand. It is a scary thing for you, there is no doubt. But then you really needn't worry," said the lawyer, gazing deep into the farmwoman's darting eyes. "We can succeed; if only we want to. We have a very strong case here, you believe me."

"Can anyone really fight JP?" said the woman, a measure of trust creeping into her gaze nonetheless at the lawyer's words.

"No one is above the law, Njambi. I know that for sure because I am a lawyer. Trust me we can bring a case against the man and win."

"I have my doubts." Njambi's gaze was trained on her dirty toes, wriggling slowly through the holes worn through the canvas tops of her shoes. "JP is a big man indeed." For a while she gnawed at her fingernail, thoughtful.

"I tell you it can be done," said the lawyer softly. "I have taken on even more powerful people and won. It is not as hard as you think."

"What if we don't succeed? He will throw me and my boy in the cells- that is for sure."

"Look, Mama Ndonga, I left my work and went to all this trouble to disguise myself," she indicated the tattered clothing. "Do you think I would have done all that if I didn't believe in the case? Perhaps you only need to take some time to think about it."

"No. I think I will take your word," said the woman at length, sighing. "I really don't have much choice, do I?" A thin mirthless smile split her dark lined face.

"No, I am afraid you don't. All it will take is a little boldness on your part and those of the workers who will agree to work with us."

The boy squatted a little distance from where they were, watching them warily, occasionally glancing over his shoulder to see if anyone was coming.

"That is very good to hear, and encouraging too. Thank you. But then," now the farmwoman looked upwards, her eyes shifting from the bended maize stalks to the lawyer "I am afraid I cannot pay you, *wakili*, even if we were to go ahead," she said, swallowing nervously. "I hear it costs a fortune to hire a *wakili*. I just don't have any money."

"Ah, that," said the lawyer with a smile. "Don't worry about that, Mama Ndonga."

"You mean you will help us for free?" said the farmwoman, astounded.

"Indeed I will. I won't charge you a cent."

"But...."

The lawyer smiled brightly at her, nodding softly. In the end the farmwoman lowered her head slowly, the embarrassment that had been there earlier giving way to wonderment. "I don't believe this," she whispered.

"*Niguo*, Njambi, it is true," said the lawyer firmly. "All you need to do is avail as much information as you can to me to enable me prepare a strong case."

"Well, so what do we do then?" said the farmwoman at length, admiration in her eyes.

"Thank you. This is what we must do, and urgently...."

***

When the lawyer sneaked out of the farm later that evening she had made a tour of not just most of the farm and the factory but Kampi Nyasi as well. She had seen the lad who had been beaten by the guards and had a long talk with his mother, who was naturally apprehensive at the idea of her son standing in court to testify against JP.

"I don't want my son to end up in a roadside trench with a smashed skull," the mother had flatly refused. "We have seen far too many injuries on this farm already."

But with a little persuasion of the women, who had gathered in the hut on hearing the whispered news that there was a lawyer in the village she had seen the need for it. Her only concern was that if JP were convicted then they would all be out of a job.

"Unless you stand up against the wrongs that are done against you, then soon you will have to burry someone on this farm," the lawyer had said coolly, eyeing the ring of women in the smoky hut. "I am certain that you have buried scores already due to injuries and illnesses caused by working on this farm."

"*Eeni!*" mumbled a few of the women, nodding thoughtfully.

"And I can assure you, mama, that soon you may have to burry this very son you are shielding. And by then, you can have my word, you will be too scared to say a thing against the man."

"She speaks the truth," assented another woman at the back of the gathering. "Those guards are sure going to kill someone."

"No, some *people*," added another. "If this goes on a while longer we'll be burying a number of people in this very Kampi Nyasi. The man and his guards have become like mad dogs on the prowl ever since the strike! The *wakili* is right."

There was a general assent to the statement.

"But he is my only son," the woman who's son was injured said stubbornly. "His father left this house to work the quarries in Maai-Mahiu, and we have never heard a word from him since- not even a letter. And so, what do you think I will do without my Githinji? No, I shall not have my son beaten up by JP's *mikora* while I can help it!"

"Instead you'll let him nurse his injuries in this little hut that is fit for housing JP's dogs and do nothing about it, is that what you are saying?"

By then most of the women gathered in the hut had been swayed over, and one by one they grunted their assent for something to be done against JP and his goons. After all he had put Wangari in the cells, or hadn't he? Wasn't that evidence enough that the man was a crook who was up to no one's good?...

Eventually the woman had reluctantly given in,

even agreeing to let his son be taken to the mission hospital the following day to have his injuries examined and the doctor give his report.

It is the Police station that she flatly refused to approach, a shadow of fear creeping into her eyes at the suggestion that she goes to report the matter in order to obtain a P3 form. The same fright came into the eyes of the lad, who all the while had been watching from the lumpy sway-backed donkey bed set up against the wall, his head propped up on a folded gunny sack, watching the visitors with detached stoicism.

"You don't expect her to go to the Police now, do you?" supplied someone at the back of the gathering, echoing everyone else's fear. "Certainly not after the same were used against us just the other day? No, I don't think she should go there."

There were murmurs of approval all around the smoky hut.

But it was the tale that Ndonga's mother told as she escorted her through the maize field on her way out that shocked the lawyer the most. They had to stop for a while in the wattle trees for her to take in the details of the rape, her eyes widening as the account unfolded.

As for Njambi, her trust in the woman strengthened by the events of the day and the resolution of the women in the village to do something to improve their lot, she poured it all out like she had never told anyone. It was a strange comfort that she read in the steadfast gaze of the lawyer, which was trained on her throughout the account. She nodded slowly, encouraging, until in the fullness of it even she couldn't stop a tear that had been glistening in the corner of her eye rolling slowly down her cheek.

"Here, feel me," said Njambi in a charged whisper, no longer concerned about spilling it all out. "You are a woman just like me. Feel my belly here. I know when things are not right with my body, *Wakili*. I think it might even have been far much more than just the brutal act."

When the lawyer eventually crawled through the *panya* opening and back to the by then darkening road, her head was milling with thoughts and plans. On top of that she was seething with a cold rage deep inside. It had been a long day of many unpleasant discoveries.

***

When Miss Nyokabi finally got home she found the phone ringing. She had lived long enough with the instrument to know when it had been ringing the whole day- there was a strain in the shrill bell that revealed its fatigue when she listened closely. What she badly needed at that time was a long soak in a hot herbal bath.

Flicking the light switch she kicked off her ridiculous pair of canvas shoes and went into the hall to take the call.

"Hello, Julia. I suppose you are feeling very good with yourself right now, eh? With hardly a care in the world what happens to your scheduled appearances in court today, huh?" Mark K'Opiyo's flat baritone had this way of making her feel like a little girl on the receiving end of the science master's lecture.

"Hey, Mark, I thought 'Good Evening' was the civil thing to say to a lady at this time of day!" said Ms Nyokabi with a laugh.

"That, my fine lady, would apply only where the

courtesy is mutual. Where have you been, Julia? And, honestly, don't you think it's time you invested in a cell phone?"

"That I am seriously considering, Mark. As for where I've been it's a long story. I don't even suppose you'd want to be seen with me at dinner in the state I am in right now- leave alone introduce me to your friends."

"Julia, I thought that one of the policies of this company was to let your partner know where you were at all times, not to mention shouldering your share of the baggage."

"That's right. Still, we are allowed once in a while to bend the law, aren't we? The basis of Law is that it is pliant- it is not cast out of cement. At least I remember that from my training."

"I don't like this at all, Julia." There was a pause at the other end in which the click of Mark's Zippo lighter sounded as he lit one of his awful-smelling cigars that had accompanied him home from his postgraduate studies in Russia. "I demand an explanation. You know, in all honesty, I don't even know how I ever got mixed up with such a character as you, Julia."

"You know what they say about opposites? Often they don't even know they click- until an outsider points it out. Look, Mark, I am not in a position to give a full brief right now, but the truth is I didn't spend the whole day in bed. I was doing some serious work on one important personality."

"I hope it pays your share of the bills and compensates for lost business."

"That I am not so sure of."

"Why? You said it is a job you are doing, didn't you?"

Miss Nyokabi swallowed, picturing the scowl on her partner's dark face. "That I did. But the job is for free. You see, I won't get paid a single cent."

"Julia, you know what? I think you are a nut case..."

"*Please*, Mark, if you will spare me the cynicism, I really *need* to get into my bath. But before you hang up on me there's one thing I need you to do for me. I need to talk to an expert on labour matters as pertains to employer-employee relations. I need to know what the law says on child labour and the rights of the worker. There must be a suitable NGO around that is involved in such."

"What I think you need is two more years in Law school to get answers for your dud question," said Mark with a chuckle. "They should charge you a pretty sum to run you through Vicarious Liability, Tort and the like a second time around."

"I'd like to believe that that means you'll have set up something for me before midday tomorrow. As for now, I really *must* hang up. Sweet dreams, my dear. Bye!"

Ms Nyokabi replaced the ancient receiver on the hook and sighed, only then becoming fully conscious of the clothes she was in. By God, she *stinked*.

She took off the headscarf and felt her tussled hair, half expecting tiny six-legged creatures to crawl up her wrist. She started unbuttoning the old dress, watching herself in the mirror on the wall. She vaguely wondered how her nieces would react if they were to come storming into the house right then.

For once she regretted not having a house help around to run her a hot herbal bath and fix her a quick hotplate. She was not just dirty, but also famished.

***

Njambi too had a visitor later that night. It was after they'd had their evening meal as Mukami was washing the dishes in one of the sooty *sufurias*, stacking them on a wooden rack by the fire so that they could drip onto the earthen floor. Ndonga sat on one of the fireside stools warming his feet and hands, which he had scrubbed white with the coarse round stone in the bath shelter as he took his evening bath.

"Mama, there's someone at the door," said Mukami, straightening and wiping a soap sud off her chin. She was growing into a lanky girl, rapidly coming up to Ndonga's height. Still she was getting rather too long-limbed for a girl, and dark, the object of joking remarks from her brother whenever they played in the yard behind the house.

"Ndonga, go and see who it is," said their mother from the bed against the wall, where she had already stretched out to rest her aching back. "Remember you are the man in the house now." A shadow of fear crossed her tired face nonetheless, even as she rose on her elbow. It was rather late for a visit.

"You are not asleep already, are you, Mama Ndonga?" called Juma as the door creaked open.

"Oh, I was just preparing to go to bed. It is these children who are keeping me, and yet I am so tired!" said Njambi, inviting him to sit on the folding chair.

He was wearing his worn greatcoat, and through the part in the front the shiny haft of his club that was stuck into the waistband could be seen. There was a whiff of liqueur on his breath.

"Today you didn't stay long at Mama Pima's, did you, Juma?"

"I didn't have money. And yet the woman is getting even harder on the credit with us."

215

"You don't pay her on time, that's why. Don't you know she needs to order more stock?"

"Order more stock indeed- as if we don't know of the brewery she runs in the marshes down by the overgrown end of the valley," said Juma, biting hard on the splayed white stick he was chewing and spitting on the floor between his spread feet.

Ndonga swung back the bent nail that secured the door and resumed his place by the fire.

"I think you are a little too old to sit by the fire, Ndonga," said Juma, eyeing him scornfully. "You must be getting ill-mannered pampered day to day by the women here."

"Aah! *Wacha!*" said Ndonga, waving the finger of his good hand at him.

"I have warned the boy occasionally to stop sitting in the woman's place. But he just doesn't listen," said Njambi, bringing down a mug to pour the visitor some of the brown tea in the teapot. "And yet he is coming of age. Soon I will be taking him down to the river to have his foreskin nipped off."

The boy's sister laughed, covering her mouth behind her hand.

"You should bring him over to my place. I wouldn't mind some male company at night."

"Is that where the talk was leading?" said Njambi, pausing. "In that case, then I think it is *you* who needs to invite someone to come and live properly with you; and not this child. Don't you see the years are passing you by? Or don't you ever look in the mirror and see those grey hairs popping up in your sideburns?"

"Oh, Mama, Juma doesn't even own a mirror!" said the boy, even as he burst into laughter together with his sister.

"*Shhhh*! Don't you two laugh so loud!" said their mother, drawing the old shawl closer about her shoulders and sitting down on the bed. "Don't you see we are right next to JP? You don't want him storming in right now, do you?"

After Juma had finished the tea he rose to leave.

"Eh? So soon?" said Njambi, surprised. "I thought we would trade some fireside gossip to bring sleep closer."

"It's late. I must go to my place and see if I can fix myself something."

"Sorry we had finished all the food," she said, indicating the empty *sufurias* by the fire. "Today your drawing pots got here after the rain had ended."

"It is alright."

As she saw him to the door he called her aside into the night. She was hardly surprised. He had appeared preoccupied, and it was plain this was not just another routine visit.

"Mama Ndonga, who was that woman you were with today?" he said after they were out of the hearing of the children, speaking in lowered tones, conscious of the farm-owner's house close by.

"Ah, *that*? She was just a friend, why?"

"Don't lie to me. I've never seen her on the farm. And I was not for once fooled that she's just another ordinary farm worker, despite her tattered dress."

"And just how does an ordinary farm worker look like?" said Njambi doggedly, needing to know why he was asking after her.

"Look, Mama Ndonga, I know for sure that she was up to something. And indeed I followed her around for some time. Truly that is partly the reason why I didn't stop or question her, right from when she showed up

217

in the morning. I need to know what she was up to talking to the women of Kampi Nyasi."

There was a hint of fear in his voice that was clearly discernible, even in the enveloping dark.

"You have been sleuthing around, haven't you, Juma?"

He remained silent, waiting.

"You are not scared, are you?" said Njambi softly, moving closer.

He still did not answer.

"No need for you to admit it. I know you are. I can feel it." Njambi sighed, measuring her words, conscious of how strained their relationship had become ever since the day of the riot and the ensuing clamping-down by the farm owner. Her ears were cocked to pick out one of the night guards snooping about in the yard.

In the adjoining chicken-house the two-day-old chicks that had been brought earlier that day clucked on like a choir of crickets, rummaging through the feed. The light from the overhead bulbs that were left on throughout the night to keep them warm escaped through the chinks in the planks in the wall, attracting swarms of night insects.

"You are right, Juma. She was no ordinary Chapa Kazi-type worker."

"I knew. She was a spy, wasn't she?" he said fearfully, his tall frame growing rigid with tension.

"No, she was on no spying mission."

"Well...?"

"I don't know if I should tell you this, Juma," said Njambi, uncertain.

"I am waiting," said Juma softly. "I will find out sooner or later anyway."

"I guess you will too." Njambi paused, swallowing, her eyes seeking the visitor's in the dark. "She is a lawyer, Juma. She is going to help us bring a case against JP in court."

There was an audible gasp as Juma's breath held. The silence that followed was weighty, the matured tension tangible in the thick canvas of night.

"A lawyer you say?" whispered Juma at length, his voice a pitch higher, like a boy who had stumbled on a well-kept family secret.

"Yes, a lawyer, Juma," said Njambi calmly, crossing her arms over her chest.

"You want to take JP to court?"

"Yes."

"You are sure about this, Mama Ndonga?"

She let the question hang, eyeing him steadily in the dark. There was another brief silence as the information sunk, the gears in Juma's thought process cranking almost audibly.

"It is scary, isn't it?" said Njambi softly. "You don't believe it?"

"But....?" He could not find the words to complete the sentence.

"It scared me too when it was first suggested to me," said Njambi in the patient tone of the village pastor charged with a band of country miscreants. "But now that I've thought about it, I think it's the right thing to do. We cannot continue to live in the shadow of fear all our lives."

"You know that the consequences could be grave, Mama Ndonga," said Juma cautiously, yet to come to terms with the implications of what he had heard. "You know that it could turn against you, and that a lot of people could be in trouble for it."

"I know that. And it is not just I. We *all* are fully conscious."

"There are a number of you involved in this, is it?" said Juma fearfully, his trembly voice cracking.

"That is right."

"You really don't want to take on such a foe as JP for a duel, do you, Mama Ndonga?"

"I was scared too initially, as I've just told you." There was a calmness about Njambi that surprised even herself. She moved her hand lower and touched her belly, feeling the little bulge through the thin fabric of her *lesso*. For a while there she debated whether to tell him. So far only the lawyer and herself knew about it. It had been most frightening to her in the second month, and days on end she had agonized over how she would handle it. Especially given the circumstances that had given rise to it, and which had remained a dark secret in the recesses of her mind, tightly lidded. She was yet to come fully to terms with it.

"You know, Njambi, I really don't think that this is a light matter at all," said Juma, his hands buried in the patch pockets of his old coat. "I-I don't know what to say," he ended with a shake of the head.

"You don't have to say anything, Juma. At least not tonight."

"You know that we have lived on this farm for many years, Mama Ndonga."

"I know."

"That all your children were born here, right on this Chapa Kazi, Mama Ndonga."

"I know that too."

Juma paused, as if in a stutter. "You know, there

are other ways to go about this thing...I am certain...."

"Juma!" the snap in her voice rang with an authority she had never used even with him. He clammed up, fidgeting nervously on his feet.

"It is good you came, Juma," said Njambi at length, swallowing. "And I have told you this not because you asked. I intended to inform you still, after I had mulled over it tonight. I don't expect you to join in. But more important I don't expect you to share a word of it with anyone else. You know what that will mean. You were my husband's best friend when he was still with us. And that has not changed, even with his passing." She paused yet again, swallowing. Suddenly she raised her face, a grave look in her eyes even in the dark. "Go now. Go and sleep."

Juma gazed for a while at Yakobo's widow in the hazy light of night, not quite sure he was looking at the same person he had known before.

When he turned to go his legs were shaking, heart thumping inside his chest with the frightening aftershock.

She watched him for a while until he had disappeared into the cover of the tall maize. Then she turned and went back in to bed.

Chapter Twenty Two

IT was in the second week after they had started the evidence-gathering process. They were driving slowly along the rut-marked road, the lawyer at the wheel of her seven-year-old Toyota. There was a measure of excitement in the car. The officer from the Ministry of Labour, a thin balding man who had initially reserved his doubts about convicting such a person as JP was upbeat, chatting excitedly with the other officer from the children's court seated beside him in the back. They had just successfully served JP with the court order after days of playing cat-and-mouse. It had been a tiring-sometimes nakedly perilous- two weeks of investigations at Chapa Kazi Farm indeed, which saw them occasionally sneak in under the cover of dark, risking the guards' poisoned arrows, to gather evidence.

"We are going to nail him," said the labour officer, nodding confidently. "I am certain the best lawyers in the world won't get him off this hook."

"Indeed," said the other officer. "As matters stand now, JP faces a charge sheet a mile long. The man is staring a real long jail term in the face."

"You are certain he won't bail himself out?" said the labour officer to the lawyer upfront. "The man has the money and the influence, you know."

"...Hmmm...That's a possibility," said the children's officer, a shadow crossing her face. "He would certainly influence the rest of the investigations that have to be done."

"I don't think so," said Ms Nyokabi, starting the wipers to clear the windscreen. "He will certainly try, there is no doubt. But I don't see him succeeding. It is the rape case that will do him in, both legally and politically. I am certain we can push it successfully in court. On top of that I am saving the boy for last. I plan to push for him to appear before the court, even if in camera, and have him bare his mangled hand. That will certainly punch a huge hole in JP's defense, if not drive the last nail in his coffin. The witnesses we've lined up have assured us they will testify. Of all of them, it is the juvenile's testimony that is going to pull it in for us. It has a lot of weight, as our friend here will agree."

"I am especially keen on that," said the children's officer, cradling her patent leather handbag in her lap. "You don't know half the horror I felt when I looked at that boy's hand."

"It looks horrible," agreed the lawyer. "The man is a beast. You should have listened to his mother's account of the rape. It moved me to tears."

"I hope all our witnesses cooperate. JP certainly wields a lot of influence out here, you know."

"We must keep our fingers crossed," said the children's officer. "Still I am very positive about this. The time we put in was not in vain."

"Well, let's hope nothing happens before D-day, Monday. I am certain the case will draw lots of publicity," said the labour officer.

"You can be sure it will be splashed all over the front pages," said the lawyer, smiling confidently. "Already some guys from the dailies have been hanging around our office. I don't know how they got wind of it. Mark is doing a splendid job wetting their appetites too. We will certainly need the publicity during the long trial."

"JP is not just another maize-roasting Njoroge on the street you know. That certainly was to be expected. And *you*, Ms Nyokabi, will be right in the pop of the flashbulbs," said the children's officer.

"Hey, we are in this together, don't you forget!"

The rough road straightened out into a level stretch as they passed the last of the tall wattle trees lining the farm. Suddenly Ms Nyokabi glanced in the driving mirror and saw the olive-green Range Rover loom up behind them. It was the same car that had been parked in the drive of the palatial farmhouse just that morning. It was being driven at speed, and was coming straight into their rear.

"Seems like we have company," said the labour officer, jerking his thumb at the rear-view mirror.

"I've seen it," said Ms Nyokabi, a crease appearing on her forehead.

"Our friend JP is definitely not out on a leisure drive through the farmlands," said the children's officer, twisting around in the seat. She reached into her handbag for her cell phone and hurriedly placed a call to an unmarked Police car that, as prearranged, was patrolling the area.

"I figured things wouldn't run so smoothly," she said, a nervous edge in her voice.

A strong companionship had grown between the three of them during the two weeks they had been working on the case, a sense of purpose that could only be sattisfied by successful completion of the case.

***

Back at the farmhouse JP's wife Njeri was in a rage. She was standing over the torn pieces of the court order that were scattered on the thick brown carpet, her arms planted on her hips, seething. The news had just killed her appetite for the roast goat ribs on steamed potato the cook had prepared for her.

"*Stupid!*" she hissed, stamping down on the torn order. "You people don't know who you are joking with!"

In her rage her eyes had narrowed, drawing back into their sockets, her heavily made-up face turning the colour of beet around the cheeks and brow. There was droll on her trembling penciled lips.

In a huff she headed for the mini bar and poured herself a stiff Scotch, barely keeping her hands steady. She walked out of the dining room through the French windows onto the rooftop terrace that overlooked the farm.

She drank slowly, her face puckering as the searing drink traveled down her gut and hit the pit of her stomach. She poured another slug and this time tossed it back, her eyes watering.

"*Jinga!*" she snarled at the swaying tattered tops of the banana trees beneath. "*Ngui!*"

Moving towards the balustrade she clamped her heavily adorned hand on the rail and looked out towards the swathe of brown on the periphery that was Kampi Nyasi, her eyes darkening. "You and your stupid friends had better win this, big Toto," she whispered softly, a callous smile disfiguring her face at the memory of the man whimpering on the phone just a while back. "Yes, you had better win this. Otherwise you are finished!"

Then she threw the whisky bottle over the side.

It sailed through the air and bounced off the tile roof, breaking on the cobblestones down beneath. It barely missed a servant who was returning from the kitchen with a laden tray.

***

The Range Rover bared on them, headlights flashing. Ms Nyokabi swung the little Toyota to the roadside as she caught a mean look on the face of the driver of the Range Rover, J.P. King'ong'o, clearly reflected in her rear-view mirror. The Toyota banged into a rut as the Range Rover drew level and the farm owner leaned out, a venomous look on his moist face.

"You are dead people!" he snarled as he wrenched suddenly on the wheel and the Range Rover slammed sideways into the smaller Toyota, forcing it off the road.

On the other side, beyond the thin hedge, the ground gave away suddenly, dropping into a deep gorge, a fall of about sixty feet into the tree-covered valley. He had chosen his assault well.

Ms Nyokabi slammed on the brakes and the Range Rover eased off, sliding forward and swerving to the far end with an angry grind of metal against metal.

But it was only for a while. Soon it swung back into the road, coming in for another assault. This time the wrought iron bulbar caught the little car in the ribs and butted, dragging it along. Ms Nyokabi instinctively stepped on the brakes, fighting the car. But it was like a heap of tin caught on the rail by the train. The Range Rover grunted on, unhindered by the little car's struggle, and sent it shooting into the hedgerows.

That was shortly before the white Peugeot wagon appeared further down the road. And as the Peugeot swung across and screeched to a stop yards from the scene, four Police officers leapt out, their drawn guns trained on the Range Rover's cabin.

"It's over now, JP!" shouted the senior officer, his revolver leveled at the window of the humming Range Rover. "*Kwisha!* You had better give yourself up!"

Chapter Twenty Three

THE last of the construction workers finished their lunch and ambled out of the kiosk back to their work at the new site on Mombasa Road. And as they left, the proprietor of the place took stock of their entries in the little 'credit' book that she kept locked away in a drawer in the inner room. She carefully made a total of the entries in each row, using a small electronic calculator and entered them in red biro in the ruled line in the column. She had to be careful with the accounting because she needed to meet her daily target for the revolving fund her women group had set up.

The following day would be payday, and she made a note to be at the gate of the site early to catch those who might want to default. There had been a few cases in the past month who had since quit working at the site, and who had taken off without settling their bills running into thousands.

In the yard outside her two helping hands were busy washing the dishes in the huge plastic tubs filled with warm soapy water, stacking them on the wooden rack constructed beside to dry. It had been a busy day, and sales had been good.

In the shade of the acacia tree in the yard her children played with the potato chipper, trying to get it to slice up a strange-looking fruit.

"You will ruin that machine with your thick head, you Ndonga!" she shouted through the doorway. "Hurry on back to school, will you? Haven't you had your lunch?"

"We are going, Mama," said Mukami, urging her brother to lower the heavy iron arm, winking at the other girl to fetch more roots to chop. At the other end Ciiru was foraging for the rotten potatoes that had been discarded on the garbage pile, fighting off a fat black nanny goat that had strayed into the yard.

She watched them for a while, the boy specifically. There was still that troubled look in his eyes every time he approached the potato chipper. The doctor had said that it would only be a matter of time before he fully adjusted to the use of the metal arm they had fitted. Still, there was the inner struggle that he must overcome on his own. Nevertheless it was encouraging to see that he had adjusted so well at school. His class master was even considering making him prefect because of the respect he commanded among the other children, partly due to his age.

Just then a pick-up truck drew up to a stop outside and the driver leapt out, calling to one of the girls to bring his lunch of *githeri* and *chapati* as he was hungry. The children stopped their play and ran up to the truck, leaning into the open window. They were reminding the driver about their promised ride that evening after school.

"Hey, I still haven't forgotten!" said Juma, lifting the girls up in his arms. "I know you children have rather long memories. Now, go on to school. Don't you see your shadows are starting to fall on the other side of your heads?"

As the children collected their tin geometric sets and ran out of the yard Juma stooped and entered the kiosk, dangling the car keys. He was loudly complaining of the long run of deliveries he had done since morning. And still there were two more trips to make to Gikomba market.

"I say, does the whole world have to know what kind of day you had, Juma?" called Njambi through the worn netting in the doorway. "Or do you think it's only you who gets a sore back in order to earn a living?"

"*Ai!*" lamented one of the girls in the yard, "You would think he has been carrying sacks on his back all morning! And yet all that he does is sit behind the steering wheel and listen to the car radio- some people really do not appreciate when they have it so easy!"

"I say girl, watch what you say. Do you imagine driving a truck laden with sacks of *waru, mbembe* and *njahi* through the Gikomba crowds is like washing dishes?" countered Juma with a mean scowl. "You don't know half the trouble I go to getting those adamant hawkers to step out of the way to let me pass!"

Juma was always complaining. But it wasn't to say he was in any way unhappy with the job. In any case his health had improved a lot since he had left the farm and come to work here. He was much happier too.

In the inner room the baby announced her waking with a piercing cry and Mama Ndonga had to break from her accounting to go and attend to her. The baby was a healthy feeder who did not ask, but demanded. Happy Nyokabi, Njambi had named her, after the courageous lawyer who had changed their lives. And such was the brightness she had brought into their lives her siblings could hardly wait to come home from school to hold and play with her.

And as the woman stood outside the kiosk suckling her baby, watching the shadow of the overhanging acacia bough play on her cherubic cheeks, she felt a wave of immeasurable joy sweep over her. And as often happened when she got to feeling that way, she wished that Yakobo were here to witness how far they had come. Him and the good lawyer, who still came by to visit on Sundays whenever she could find the time.

Chapter Twenty Four

THE warder led them down a long grey corridor to a little waiting room that was painted the same somber colours as every building in the place. There was the feeling of entrapment as the steel doors clanged in place, which rent the place a cagey air.

They sat down on the hard benches and waited as the officer went into the annals of the prison, save for Gathoni who chose to remain standing, pacing the room with her hands clasped behind her back. Perhaps she was too nervous to remain still. They all experienced nervousness when they came to this place.

Mama Pima was looking angelic in her white Sunday dress with lacing on the collar, complete with a starched white headdress. Her face and huge hands were scrubbed and oiled, on her middle finger glinting a wedding band that no one could remember a spouse giving her. Probably it was pawned by a patron.

She was quite a contrast to the drab woman who hustled drunks for their coins in her *chang'aa* den in Kampi Nyasi.

The same white was worn by Gathoni, albeit hers was stiffer and much worn, made of the cheaper Jinja cloth and lacking the lacy frills of a more modern cut. But it was well pressed nonetheless, her worn canvas shoes scrubbed clean.

Njambi sat in dignified silence beside them, clutching the *ciondo* containing the food they had brought. She looked plumper and rounder of face as compared to those days long gone when she had worked at Chapa Kazi farm.

Unlike the previous visits their anxiety today was mixed with suppressed excitement. It was November, and December the 12th was only a few weeks away. The date when Wangari, the only one of the Chapa Kazi three still at the prison, would be discharged on Presidential decree. It had been a long two years.

As they waited, conversation kept to a bare minimum, Mama Pima reached into her white leather handbag and took out a tiny palm-sized purse made of brown calico. Usually it was kept in the little pouch that had a drawstring which hang from around her neck and was kept away in her bust next to her breast. She opened the zipper and from amidst the folded notes crammed inside took out a pressed white handkerchief. She unfolded it carefully and wiped her moist face and neck. The benefits of her long trade were obvious on her well-fed body, which would break into a sweat even on the chilliest day.

She passed the handkerchief inside her bust and wiped at her sweaty underarms, which had formed wet patches on her dress. Then she meticulously folded it back into a little triangle along the ironed fold lines, flattening it in her huge palms and returned it to the little pouch.

"It is a rather hot day," said Gathoni, gazing at a long jagged crack that ran from the ceiling down the wall, and which was unsuccessfully hidden behind a swathe of flaking plaster and peeling paint.

"*Mwana*! I wonder if someone here can spare us a drink of water."

The iron door squealed and the uniformed warden led in Wangari.

Gathoni, suddenly assuaged by emotion, rose and went into the elder woman's embrace, her eyes misting with the memory of the shared times they had

1ad together in the jail before her own release.

"You women have only fifteen minutes," said the warden n the gruff tone that everyone working here adapted, in 1er eyes the vague interest of someone who had to do an 1npleasant duty over and over. "*Malizeni haraka haraka!*"

"*Eee, Afande,*" said Mama Pima.

"*Ni wega, nyina wa Ciiru?*" asked Gathoni in greeting, 1er voice trembling with emotion.

"*Ee, ni wega,*" said the older woman, clasping her arms 1rmly around the slim Akorino woman. "*Uhoro?*"

"*Tu riega.*"

She went on to embrace Mama Pima, and lastly Njambi. The latter's embrace lasted longer, the prisoner staring steadily into her visitor's eyes.

"How is my little girl?" asked Wangari at last, her voice surprisingly calm, eyes still hard and focused, like they had always been on the farm when she gave her little speeches.

"Ciiru is fine," said Njambi, equally steadily. "She takes 1er lessons well, and is always willing to help around the 1ouse."

"That is good. I hope she is not getting naughty with you like she used to."

The prisoner paused, taking in a lungful of air. "Is her math grade getting better?"

"She tries," said Njambi, nodding. "It is still not as good. Ndonga helps her with the homework whenever he can. She likes English and History better."

"That is good. She was always giving me problems with *hesabu.* I hope the teachers at the new school are better."

A pensive look clouded the prisoner's eyes for a while as she looked beyond her visitors at the grey walls.

Wangari had grown gaunter, the hair at her temples going to grey, the crow's feet around her eyes etched. The skin on her forehead was stretched taut across her face, evenly lined with narrow furrows, as if she thought a lot. But there was still that stiffness in her upright physique that not even the prison could get to. She still radiated that air of command, that unflailing steadfastness that was almost motherly, and which had endeared her not just to her fellow inmates but to the warders as well. It was little wonder that she had been put in charge of the prisoners in her block in just the second week at the jail.

"It is good when our children get an education like this." She nodded, her eyes glazing for a while as if she was in private conversation with herself.

"How is Kampi Nyasi?" she said to Mama Pima, moving towards the bench. "Do the women still gather at the church to discuss 'welfare' on Sunday evenings after church? Are our savings projects still going on?"

Mama Pima gazed for a while at the wall, her dark moist brow lined. A cloud passed over her face and she shook her head slowly. "Kampi Nyasi is no more, Wangari. Most of the women have left, and the new ones who move in hardly stay long enough before they leave for other farms. Mostly they are young single mother's impatient to find a good life for their child. No, things have changed quite. Even my patrons are always complaining. There is no money. The life there has changed a lot."

"Is it?" said the prisoner, a look of vague surprise passing over her lined face as she digested the news.

"She speaks the truth, Nyina wa Ciiru," said Njambi.

"I see. What happened to JP?"

"JP is no more," said Mama Pima softly. "Things started going downhill for him right after he lost the case. The bank made real their threat to seize equipment on the farm over his loan defaults and they came and stripped the place bare. Now trucks and tractors no longer roar at Chapa Kazi like they used to, neither does the factory by the river hum in the night. All is quiet. Njeri and the children are never seen on the farm these days. I hear they went to America. The man is ruined. There was even talk that the farm is up for sale. I don't think it is generating enough money."

"It is true what people were saying," said the Akorino woman, sitting down next to Wangari. "The farm really belonged to Njeri and not JP. Only the land was JP's."

"I always suspected that," said Njambi, nodding.

"He-heee...! Are you people speaking of the Njeri I know or someone else?" said Wangari with a snide laugh, snapping out of her train of thought. "If it is the same Njeri of JP's, she probably has found herself a *Mzungu* lover by now in America and shrugged off the past. She was a vulture, that woman. I always knew it. For all her fashionable dressing and painted urban beauty she would gouge out her own mother's eyes if the poor woman was on her last breath!"

"You are right, Wangari," said Njambi. "That one is a money woman."

"I tell you. And I was never fooled every single day I slaved away on that farm about who the true owner of the place was. Njeri was the true owner, regardless of the fact she would never be caught dead with her pretty 'office' hands soiled by smelly manure."

"I don't think the man is going to have enough money to defend his seat come the next campaigns either," said Mama Pima.

"And it would be no surprise. That is the way a home goes when the woman leaves," said Wangari judiciously. "They never seem to learn, these men."

For a while there that remembered glow appeared in her eyes, shining brightly in the tortured depths.

There followed a moment of silence in which the prisoner clasped her face in her arms and sighed, her eyes closed. "I miss outside," she said at length, her gaze lifting from her corny chapped toes wriggling in her faded bathroom slippers. "I miss home."

For a while there a wavering appeared in her eyes, her shoulders dropping. When it passed she let go of Njambi's hand and rose, walking towards the far corner.

"Sit down and eat now, Wangari," said Mama Pima, the hoarse edge that usually instilled the fear of God in wayward drunks who were potential trouble creeping into her voice. "We brought this food for you."

Wangari gathered the brief skirts of her stripped jail frock in her lap and sat down.

The warden, who had been standing watch in the doorway all this while came forward as Njambi opened the *ciondo*. She took a look inside, rummaging among the dishes, and then withdrew.

"How is Nyina wa Mumbi?" asked Wangari after another woman who was a friend of hers, making a ball of *irio* in her hand. "Has her eye gotten any better?"

"She underwent the operation successfully," supplied Gathoni. "The doctors say she must go back for special spectacles which they ordered for her from abroad. But the twitching and pain has now stopped."

"That is good." Wangari ate in silence for a while, dipping in the soup bowl and conveying the balls of mashed food to her mouth. "I always thought the woman should have sued JP for the trouble with her eye. Wasn't it the twig of a coffee tree that struck and injured her while she was at work? I remember very well because I was working in the row next to hers that day. And now that that wonderful lawyer won the case for Njambi, perhaps she too can have a go at the old glutton."

"Yes, you are right," said Gathoni. "She too should be paid."

"But hasn't so much time elapsed since she had her injury?" said Mama Pima doubtfully.

"You, don't joke with the law!" said Wangari with a raised eyebrow. "The *sheria* can dig up a case that goes back a hundred years- if only there is need. I tell you, anything is possible in this Kenya! It is only us poor women without an education who don't know some of these things."

"You have a point," said Mama Pima, helping herself to some of the boiled *nduma*. "Remember how they dug into Njambi's case, going back to things that JP himself had probably forgotten? Maybe we should approach the lawyer and talk to her about it."

"We can offer her a fee for her troubles this time around," said Njambi, agreeing with them.

"Well, that I suppose will depend on Nyina wa Mumbi herself."

The warden, who all this while had been waiting in the corridor, now came in. "Women, I will have to cut short your talk. Your time is up now. The *mahabusu* must go back to the cells."

"Hey, but they just got here!" protested Wangari, a cunning smile on her face. "Come on, *Afande*, you can give us a minute, at least."

"Alright, wrap it up, then. Otherwise I will have the other women come in and take away that food you are toying with!" said the warden with a stern look.

Wangari rose and walked towards Njambi, taking her hand in hers. "Njambi, my friend, I know I will

soon leave this place. But I must say this to you, and
these women here are my witnesses, you have been a
wonderful friend to me. I can never repay you enough
for caring for my Ciiru while I was away. I must thank
you very much."

"But it was only my duty!" said Njambi as she was
swayed into the older woman's embrace. "You would
have done the same for me, Wangari."

Her voice trailed off as the wave of emotion
assailed her. Tears choked her before she could reveal
to the older woman about the little *mutumba* clothes
business that awaited her when she got out, and
which she had started and held in trust for her in her
absence to help her get back on her feet.

The warder had to come in and separate the two
women, leading away the prisoner firmly. And for the
first time since the women had known her Wangari
hid her face from them. Just like Njambi there were
tears glistening in her eyes.

***

In another part of the town on a hot dusty afternoon
a lean balding man dressed in a creased brown suit and
a frayed shirt that was falling apart at the collar left the
jostling River Road crowd and stepped into a narrow
dimly lit corridor. His trouser leggings were covered
with the fine grey dust of the seedier streets of that
part of town, a generous amount of which had collected
in the flap of the one-inch turn-ups. The old nylon tie
he wore loosened over his shirt was frazzled and dirty,
thin as a wick. It had a fading symbol of two crossed
axes, souvenirs of an equally faded era. The leather of
his hobnailed brown shoes was stiff and cracked, badly
in need of the services of a shoeshine boy.

In the welcome cool of the corridor he stopped and
leaned on his walking stick that had been hacked out

of a tree branch, pulling a crumpled dirty handkerchief from his pocket. Slowly he wiped his wrinkled face, passing the corner of the creased handkerchief inside his nostril to clean it. He removed his warped old Stetson, the leather of which was equally hard and cracked and scraped sweat from the dirty band with a corny split thumbnail, wiping the moisture on the seat of his pants. He was hungry and thirsty, and would have welcomed a cold mug of beer at the smoky pub further down the street. But he was out of money.

He adjusted the wide leather belt that secured the gathered folds of his oversize trousers over his caved belly, reminding himself to make another hole in the stiff leather when he got home.

He then clutched the brown envelope and the folded much-thumbed newspaper he carried under his arm and started the long climb up to the second floor, leaning on the walking stick, breathing heavily through his nose and mouth. His steps were gouty, the worn shoe-soles shuffling on the red cement.

The public secretary at the landing did not seem too enthusiastic on seeing him.

"You haven't finished the last chapter yet?" said the old man, poring over the contents of the secretary's 'IN' tray, a scowl coming to his lined face. He had a surprisingly hard voice for his condition, the bark in it commanding attention.

"I am almost through, *Mzee.*"

He eyed her acidly for a while, as if irritated by the slight. She should have said *'Mheshimiwa'*. "Well, you had better hurry up. I have a meeting with the publisher tomorrow. You are holding the whole process up with your snail's typing, woman!"

The typist nodded, rummaging in the pile of papers in her drawer.

The old man next glanced casually around the little cardboard-walled office, taking in the other customers waiting on the hard bench. And then with an air of open contempt, he opened the brown envelope and dumped a sheaf of papers on the desk.

"That should cover the most exciting face of my life with the Party!" he said, his moist face brightening. "I want it done exactly as I have written it. This is priceless information!"

The last was addressed at the mixed motley waiting on the bench.

"I want this work finished by tomorrow, woman, hear?"

The secretary nodded.

And then with a last sweeping glance around, the old man turned and limped out of the room, grunting deep inside his dewlapy chin to clear the irritating sputum lumped there.

"Who is that man?" asked one of the secretary's customers after he had left. He was a dark grey-bearded man with a huge red cross embroidered in the lapel of his faded grey suit and on his green turban. He was the pastor of a slum church in Mathare Valley there to prepare the ten-percent tithe forms for his flock.

"Don't you know him?" said the typist, lifting her mop of greasy curls that spilled over the ancient machine she was wrestling with. She had a tortured thin face and a cheerless smile that exposed only the tips of her brown teeth. "I am hardly surprised by your reaction. You know the man still believes he is the most important person around," she said with a cheerless laugh.

"What is he writing?" said the other man at the end of the queue, a young man just barely twenty there to prepare his application for a cruise-ship job that had been advertised in the local dailies.

"*Ati* his memoirs. He says the book is going to sell like *njugu karanga* when it is finally published. Well, I hope he settles my bill."

"He hasn't paid you?" said the scrawny-looking young woman seated closest to the secretary, dubbing at her running mascara in a cracked piece of mirror. She was a twilight girl who normally worked the K-Street beat evenings, and who was there to prepare a letter to her lawyer to commence legal action against a charge who had assaulted her.

"You would think he has, seeing from the way in which he commands me around. I tell you I am yet to see a single cent from him. And until I do, his work will remain right here," said the secretary, tapping the pile of stapled notes in the drawer.

"Tch! Tch!" muttered the job-seeking young man. "Some of these old *Wazee* are very strange in deed. Just like my old man back in the village. He thinks people live on authority and hot air." A round of laughter rang in the little cardboard office at the young man's words.

"You know in these hard times you must look first where your *unga* is coming from," agreed the pastor, nodding. "Even in my line of work we are often forced to compel the congregation to give their tithe generously as we too need to earn a salary to get the work of God done."

Thereafter the typist went back to her taxing job of arranging people's hopes and aspirations in their varying scrawls on the little machine, the noisy clatter banging away the missed lunch hour.

END

www.ingramcontent.com/pod-product-compliance
Lightning Source LLC
Chambersburg PA
CBHW020102030726
47498CB00006B/1900